ISBN-13: 978-0692379578
ISBN-10: 0692379576

Author website: www.loteyrose.com

The Prequel

THE EIGHTH SQUARE

When Alice was 7

Alice made her way to the Eighth Square. She'd had *quite* enough of Wonderland for one day, and it was time to go through the Looking Glass back to her own world.

However, there was a problem. Standing there in the grass, in front of the square around the Looking Glass House, was a quite tall monster, with claws and fangs and wings and huge eyes.

"Halt little girl!" the creature commanded.

Alice looked up timidly at the creature. She was trembling all over. "Excuse me, I'm Alice and I would like to go to the Looking Glass and go through it. I don't belong here, you see, and I must be getting home."

"Yes Alice, I was told you'd be coming. I'm the Jabberwock, and I am guarding the Looking Glass House. None may enter it, unless the Queen of Hearts allows it. And she specifically told me not to allow *you* to."

"But, but, I must return home! They'll be missing me."

"That is unfortunate, but the Queen will not allow it."

Alice burst into tears. "Why not?!"

He pointed a clawed finger at her eyes. "That's why. The Queen has learned of the magical properties of your tears. She would like you to pay visits to her and cry upon her face, at Her Majesty's convenience."

"What?"

"Yes, and there are others who require your tears as well. You are to make daily rounds, visiting each person or creature. Those are to be your new duties. When you are not performing them, you shall be kept chained to your desk in your own hut."

Alice couldn't believe what she was hearing. "No! She can't do that! It's a crime and she shall surely be punished! Now I say, to avoid any trouble, I *shall* pass. Forget all that silliness you spoke of."

The monstrous face of the Jabberwock took on a mournful expression. "I'm afraid not, Miss Alice. I must obey the Queen's orders."

Alice's lower lip wobbled. "But when can I go home?"

"I'm afraid Wonderland is your home now, dear Alice, unless the Queen changes her mind, and even so, she's more likely to have you beheaded than to let you go back."

Alice formed her hands into tight fists at her side. "No! She can't do that! I am a citizen of England. I shan't be kept here!" She made a break for it, running toward the Looking Glass House.

She had only taken three steps when she felt herself forcefully pulled back. The Jabberwock had caught her in his claws, lifted her up, and now cradled her in his arms as if she were a mere baby, rather than a girl of 7!

"Release me this instant you brute!"

"I shan't do that. You must return to the hut they have made for you." He sounded a little sad.

"No!" She slapped at his arms. She felt the rage she usually tried to hold back surge through her. "I'll kill you, Jabberwock! Snicker-snack!"

"Ah, that's a reference to that horrid poem. But it's about my father, not me."

Alice squirmed with fury within his arms. "With his head, he went galumphing back!"

"Yes, the poem is a lie, you must know…"

Alice righted herself in the Jabberwock's cradling arms. She lunged for his face. "I'll kill you!" But the Jabberwock held her off, holding his hand around her midsection. Alice struggled and kicked and clawed. "I shall tear out your eyes and eat them!"

The Jabberwock chuckled. "I like girls with a little fire. But I'm afraid you are no match for me."

"I will behead you like the poem! Do not sleep, for my vengeance shall rain upon you like hellfire! I am death! I will come for you, be certain of that!"

The Jabberwock chuckled. "Do you have a vorpal blade? It is the only weapon that can easily cut the flesh of a Jabberwock."

"I will get one, and then I shall... I shall..." She suddenly broke into sobs again. "Oh I'm sorry, Jabberwock. I let my anger get the best of me. You are only doing your job."

"Oh that's quite all right. I can understand the desire to go home. I often wish I could do so myself."

She stopped struggling. "And why don't you?"

"I have been banished from my tribe because I foolishly lost my vorpal blade, and also I am indebted to the Queen."

"Ah, so she controls your fate, much as she seems to have taken control of mine." She sighed.

He sighed too. "Yes, my dear. We are similar in that respect."

"I am so so sorry if I hurt your feelings. I don't know what came over me. Sometimes I get these bad thoughts."

"Well, it is quite understandable young miss. I would probably act the same if I were in your shoes."

"They say I have two of them. Goody ones."

"Pardon?"

"They say I have goody two-shoes."

"Oh, so you've attained them?"

"Huh?"

"The Goody Two-Shoes of Legend."

"I don't know what you speak of."

"Never mind, luv. Ah, there is your escort now." He pointed with his chin.

Alice looked to see one of the Queen of Heart's guard cards approaching. He looked like a human-sized card holding a spear, with legs and arms and a flattish sort of head.

"I will take her now!" the card called out.

The Jabberwock said, "You must go with him. He shall take you to your hut, where you shall await your orders." He set her gently upon the ground, then patted her head.

Alice sighed. She lowered her head and walked toward the awaiting guard card.

She turned toward the Jabberwock. "Be well, Jabberwock. I'm sorry about what I said."

"Think nothing of it." Then he looked away.

And Alice walked toward the guard card and the fate that awaited her.

THE JaBBerWocK

When Alice was 12

The Jabberwock burst through the door of the small hut, causing it to swing and bang against the wall as it jolted open.

The guard card wasn't there. Alice was there, as he expected her to be at this time of day. Her eyes met his. As she read the sheer panic within them, she momentarily forgot herself and her arm was jerked back against the chain confining her to her desk, and she grunted.

At long last, after having dragged the girl's corpse all that way, the Jabberwock felt a little hope.

For there stands Alice, he thought, *the teary-eyed savior.*

But oh, she does not realize the great power her tiny tears hold.

...And I am forbidden to tell her.

Alice's eyes shifted to the body in his clawed hand. Her eyes widened as she took in all that red—it filled the small hut with its scent. "What happened?!" she shrieked. "Did you kill her?!"

He was dragging the little girl's corpse into the room, being careful not to be too rough. He regretted he couldn't carry her, but his right arm had been severely damaged during the fight. He said, "I didn't have a choice. She attacked me." He shook his head. "Honour dictated." He dragged the body to the desk.

He let go of Laricia's arm.

He felt feeble in front of young Alice, for she held the only chance of fixing this, in those eyes. "Please, you must try to…" He'd almost said "revive", but the Queen of Hearts had given strict orders that Alice mustn't be informed of the power of her tears. He floundered a moment for another word. "…help her," he stammered.

She shrank away from the body before she composed herself. "Help? How can I help? I'm not a doctor! Why didn't you go to the Queen?"

And he searched his mind for a deception of some sort—he couldn't tell her that if she cried on the dead girl it just might bring her back to life. He had to come up with a lie.

The girl had approached him, holding the trombone case, with a huge smile on her face.

The Jabberwock was at his post, guarding the Eighth Square, sitting in the grass, as usual. He usually only left to attend Alice's unbirthday parties every day.

"Jabberwock!" she shouted.

She was a girl of about 10, wearing a tunic and trousers. The girl's blond hair reminded him of how Alice's used to look before she started wearing it black.

He stood rigidly and crinkled his clawed fingers. The girl didn't look dangerous, but one could never be quite sure. The Looking Glass House in the square was, of course, where the Looking Glass was, and sometimes people or creatures tried to pass through it into the outside world, although as far as anyone knew, only Alice herself could actually do so.

The girl waved with a huge smile on her face and the Jabberwock cautiously waved back.

As she approached, the girl called out, "I am a musician! I wish to play for you!"

"Oh? What is your name girl? And why do you want to play for me?"

The girl was standing in front of him now. "Why, to thank you for all your good service. I apologize for putting you on the spot. I do so love to play for an audience. I practice my trombone constantly. I'm not the greatest, but I'm improving." She looked down shyly. "I look forward to someday maybe being good enough to knock 'em dead, with my music, so to speak. And...we are connected through a common acquaintance. I wanted to meet you in person." She looked up and met his eyes again.

He peered at her. Something about her was unsettling him—her smile was wide, but something was off. "You do look vaguely familiar, but I can't remember exactly how. I apologize. What is your name? You said we had a common acquaintance?"

"Yes, and no need to apologize. I'm sure us humans must all look the same to you, anyway." And she gave him a playful smirk.

He grinned back, while trying to maintain his cool. "Oh no no," he said. "For even though I'm a jabberwock, I can tell you're a prettier human than most."

The fact was that human girls weren't pretty to him and seeing one only brought back memories of his mother singing to him "little-girl's-goodbyes" to lull him to sleep with the soothing lyrics of dismembering little girls. Alice was also a little girl he wanted to dismember, but it was forbidden to kill her…but this girl… But he quickly banished the thought from his mind, for it would be dishonourable to attack without being provoked.

The girl was reacting to his compliment, saying, "Awww, that's so sweet! Well I'll tell you who our common acquaintance—hey wait! I just noticed something! How come you don't have a vorpal blade? Aren't all you jabberwock guys supposed to carry one?"

His shoulders slumped. "Yes, well the vorpal blade that was to be passed on to me was stolen."

"Stolen? Oh my! Did you ever find out who took it?"

"Yes I did. And I killed him, but I was unable to recover the sword."

"Oh wow! You killed him! But he was a human. Humans can usually only fight a jabberwock with a vorpal blade. It's the only material able to pierce their hide, right?"

He nodded. "Yes, but we didn't battle because I found out he had used deception to gain the sword, and he killed my father dishonourably as well." Something nagged at his mind. "Wait, did I ever tell you he was a human?" he asked, referring to the man who'd killed his father.

Her smile lessened. "Do you have any idea where your father's vorpal blade might be?" She kneeled beside the case.

"Wait, you're not telling me..." He watched her trembling fingers unlatch the case. She brought out the sword and took it in her hand, held it beside her face as she fixed him with a mockingly sweet smile.

"I recognize it," he said quietly.

Her voice took on a sinister tone. "Yes, this is your father's sword right here. You see, that man who slayed your father, who you then cowardly killed in cold blood when he was unarmed—that man was *my* father. My name is Laricia, daughter of Herbert the Jabberwock Slayer. I have been training for years with this vorpal blade and I am here to avenge my father. Prepare to die."

The Jabberwock's eyes pinged side to side as his mind desperately searched for a lie. He had to tug at Alice's heartstrings somehow, and immediately. Ah, he knew something guaranteed to make the waterworks flow: "She said she had to see you, even if it was her last act. Alice, she is your sister..."

Her chain clattered as she jerked, then her eyes were desperately roving the dead girl's face. "But she is the wrong age! She's not my older sister, for sure, but she's too old to be my younger sister."

She looked to the Jabberwock with pleading, desperate eyes that were already growing moist.

Excellent, he thought. *Now I need only push her...and those tears...over the edge. It shouldn't be too hard—the girl is so pathetically gullible.*

He said, "Yes, well the flow of time works differently between this world and the outside. Perhaps she's not completely gone and can yet be saved. Perhaps if you spoke to her, she might still hear?"

"Sister?" she said it as a whisper and her whole body was shaking. "My little sis?" She looked down at the corpse's face. "Why, the last time I saw her...saw you, she was just a baby. I don't even recognize her...I mean you. Sister, can you hear me? Oh, my little sis! Please say you're okay!" She awkwardly caressed the corpse's bloody cheek with her unchained hand, and here it happened. Alice burst into tears!

A huge grin stretched the Jabberwock's face before he remembered himself and struggled to suppress it.

She was sobbing and hyperventilating. "Please, my little sis! You can't be dead! Can you hear me?! Talk to me!" she shrieked. Many of her tears dropped into the red blood, mixing into pinkened dribbles.

Alice in her misery pressed her face down against the corpse's, their noses pressed together while she held her chained arm out to the side. "Please! Did you come here to meet me?! Well, then speak! As your big sister, I demand it!"

I mustn't let her know the power of her tears. He began to move toward the body.

Alice rose up on her knees. "Quit acting! Wake up. I command you!"

The Jabberwock gently clasped the dead girl's wrist. "I'm sorry. It's too late. She's gone." He began pulling the body away.

"No, don't take her!" Alice shouted in her anguish. "Where are you taking her?!"

And the Jabberwock felt that pesky emotion of guilt come over him again. He felt burdened by the things he couldn't tell her. He gave her his lame excuse—"I'm sorry, but it's too late. It's not good for her to stay here. I must take her away."

He looked to the corpse's face for any sign of movement, the chest for any rising. If her eyes opened before he dragged her out of the room, it would be a disaster, because the Queen would surely have his head for letting Alice find out the power of her tears.

Alice strained at her chain like a rabid dog. "No, you can't take her! I must say my goodbye! She must have a funeral!"

But the Jabberwock didn't reply or meet her eyes, merely kept dragging that body. As he pulled it through the door, Alice screeched, "Where are you taking her?! No!"

He pulled the body away from the hut and into a nearby forest. None of the windows of the hut faced this direction, so Alice wouldn't be able to see any of this.

Partway into the forest, it began to happen. He felt the pulse begin in her wrist. Then she took a few shallow breaths.

He dropped her wrist. He'd carried her far enough.

From the girl's pocket, he brought out the scrawny human-sized quill pen and notepad he'd stolen from Alice's desk and began writing his note—he had no ink, so he used blood.

He saw her eyelids begin to flutter, and felt relief. Here was the secret revealing itself—Alice's tears could revive the dead.

The girl named Laricia swayed the vorpal sword back and forth.

He raised his hands. "Please, there was no wrong in the way I killed your father. You don't know all the circumstances." *And in fact he deserved to die like a dog,* he wanted to add.

"I know all I need to know. You killed him in cold blood when he wasn't even armed."

She swung at him and the blade swooshed through the air. He had to jerk backward to avoid being hit.

He said, "Please, according to the rules of honour, I was obligated to avenge my father in that manner." He couldn't understand why he didn't want to fight her. Shouldn't he be happy for the opportunity?

She swung again and he just barely avoided being hit. "By striking down an unarmed human?!" she snarled.

"Yes, because he stole the vorpal blade by dishonest means."

She unleashed a savage flurry of attacks. It took extreme effort and luck to avoid her blows—she was highly skilled.

"I heard of the coin toss!" she said while she paused to catch her breath. The blade lowered slightly in her hands. "He won this sword that way, fair and square!" She raised her sword back up.

He shook his head. "No, he cheated. He used a double-headed coin."

"Liar!" she shouted, then began attacking again.

He wasn't entirely successful avoiding the swings this time—one blow stuck hard against his right arm, cutting deep, rendering it useless.

The blood ran down his arm as they stood staring at each other. "It's true. And he killed my father dishonourably, when his eyes were closed."

"What kind of idiot closes his eyes on an armed foe?"

"It was when my father handed the sword over to him. My father was bound by my dishonourable bet. I had lost the coin toss, and so he was obligated to honour the terms—he handed over the sword, but he was so overwhelmed with sorrow and shame, that he lowered his head and closed his eyes. While he was lost in his shame at my behavior, your father took advantage and beheaded him."

Her stance wavered. "No, he killed him in a great battle."

The Jabberwock huffed. "Because he said so? Because they made a poem about it that said it was so? But I was there. I saw it with my own eyes."

She made a half-hearted jab that he easily dodged. "I should believe a filthy lying jabberwock? If you saw it, why didn't you stop it?"

"I was chained to a pole because I couldn't be trusted to watch without doing anything. I was very impulsive in those days."

She stood watching him, her face showed confusion as she tried to process her thoughts. She smirked. "So you watched your father lose the fight, watched him get beheaded?" She gave another half-hearted swing at him that he dodged, but then he stumbled—his arm was still bleeding profusely and he felt dizzy from the blood loss.

He said, "They didn't fight. I guess your father went back to his village and said he fought a heroic battle, which is why they wrote that poem about him."

"My father wouldn't do that. You're the liar."

No, everything the Jabberwock said was true, but could he convince *her*?

"Please believe me—it's why I killed him the way I did, because he dishonourably murdered my father, and he cheated in order to attain the vorpal blade."

"Ha! Cheated how?"

"When he made the bet with me."

"Yes, tell me more about the bet." She took a step back, momentarily halting the battle. "I don't know much about it."

So the Jabberwock began to tell the tale, despite how ashamed he was of it. "Back then, as I said, I was impulsive. I had a gambling...problem that he took advantage of. He had a coin with his own portrait on it. He said if he flipped it and it landed on heads, he'd win the vorpal blade, which still belonged to my father, but I was almost to the age when he would give it to me."

"Oh, what was *your* prize?" she asked still holding her sword up, but it looked as if it was growing heavy in her arms despite how light vorpal blades were.

"Hmmm?"

"I've never known what you might have won in the coin toss..."

"Oh, a magical lute that could be played without having to practice on it."

"Okay, so you wanted to be a musician without having to work for it and he took advantage of your gambling problem, and you lost your bet. So what?"

"He cheated."

"According to you."

"I have proof."

She looked on blankly and lowered the sword tip onto the ground, resting her arms. "What proof?"

"I still have the coin."

"Ha! You have a coin. So what?"

"I'll bring out the coin." He slowly bent toward a chest on the ground and she tensed. "Don't worry. Let's say that we are on a temporary truce, okay? It would be dishonourable for me to attack you now. Jabberwock's honour, I just want to get the coin."

"Yes, you jabberwocks and your honour." She rolled her eyes, but she kept her arms down in an undefended position.

After some rummaging, he brought out the coin—it was a novelty coin, with the head of Herbert the so-called Jabberwock Slayer etched in it and it even had a date, of five years earlier, the year that it had all occurred.

He offered to toss it to her, but she shook her head, so all he could do was explain, once more telling the truth. "I'll tell you how I got it. See, after he beheaded my father, he walked up to me. I wanted to attack him right then, but the chains prevented me. He brought out this coin. He said he would flip it and if it landed on tails, he would cut the chains and we would have an honourable battle."

"And if it landed heads?"

"He would leave me there."

"That's ridiculous. Why would anyone make such a wager?"

"You'll see… He told me it was the same coin he'd used when he won the sword. He flipped it and it came up heads. He left the coin on the ground to mock me, then with my father's head, he went galumphing back."

"Did you ever escape?" she said with a sneer.

"Yes, I was found a few hours later and freed. And that's when I picked up the coin and discovered he had cheated."

"Oh?" she said with a smirk, but she seemed less certain now.

"Yes, because the coin is double-headed. He cheated to gain that sword you hold."

"I don't believe you."

"It is the truth. I swear to it."

"Toss it to the ground here." She pointed down with the sword and he tossed it down.

She bent to look at it. "It is my father's face, and that year, is the year of his death." She flipped the coin over with the tip of her sword. "No, no, this is a fake."

"Why would I go through the trouble of that? No, it is the coin he used. That's why, according to our code, he did not deserve an honourable death. I hunted him down and killed him, though he was unarmed, but I was unable to recover my vorpal blade. He didn't have it upon his person."

She chuckled morosely. "That's because he had it stored away. I, as his only child, inherited it. I have been training all these years, studying the art of sword wielding, studying the ways of you…jabberwocks…and your code of honour."

The Jabberwock didn't like the sound of where this was going. "Please, I believe you are an honourable warrior seeking to preserve the reputation of your father. But all I have told you is the truth. You have fulfilled your duties as a daughter. Let us go our separate ways."

"And what about the sword?"

"I respectfully ask that you return it to me, its rightful owner, for it was stolen from me by trickery."

"Well it seems we have a bit of a problem. Are you willing to let me walk out of here, taking your precious vorpal blade with me?"

For several moments, the Jabberwock thought upon it. He sighed. "If you choose to. I tell you again, all I've said has been true, and I'd like you to return my blade to me, but I respect your decision, and I truly don't wish to fight you. I…respect you." The Jabberwock was surprised himself to hear himself say that.

"Ha! So you are both a liar and a coward!"

"I did not lie."

"Well I admit, maybe I don't know the whole story, and perhaps my father wasn't perfect. But he was *my* father, and you took him from me. The blood debt must be repaid."

"I will not fight you. What can I do—"

"Oh shut up, won't you?! We *will* do battle, because I have been studying your jabberwock code. And I invoke my right of child's retribution. You killed my father so I challenge you to a duel to the death."

The Jabberwock tried to hide his surprise that a human would know the ways of the jabberwock code. He tried not to be patronizing as he said, "Do you realize what you're saying?"

She met his eyes with a cold intense stare. "Yes, the debt shall not be settled until one of us is dead." She raised her sword—it was her sword for now, but if he defeated her, it would become his—and she said, "Prepare to die."

She charged toward him with a yell and swung at his leg.

The Jabberwock no longer had a choice. He was now bound by the code to fight her to the death. He could no longer show her any mercy.

They squared off. The girl swung again, lightly cutting his left arm. She was highly skilled—a worthy opponent, especially with the vorpal blade, comprised of a charmed metal that easily sliced jabberwock flesh.

But she was growing fatigued. The vorpal blade wasn't very heavy but she was just a little girl...

He feinted to her right. When she moved her blade to parry the blow, he moved inside and slashed her arm to the bone, severing tendons and rendering her left hand useless. As she struggled to readjust to a one-handed grip, he smacked the blade out of her hand.

She met his gaze with a wide-eyed look of terror.

Then with a twinge of sorrow, he impaled her with his claws and drew upward. Her torso became drenched in red.

He withdraw his claws, and watched her, wary of any desperate last attack she might launch.

She began to cough up blood. A look of confusion came over her face, then she looked down at her mangled body.

Then she collapsed and was still.

And the Jabberwock became filled with guilt. He didn't know why he felt that way, but it was overwhelming.

"Oh god," he mumbled, then launched into action. He had to act fast. He felt for her pulse—there was none, and she wasn't breathing. They had fought to the death, honourably, and the blood debt had been settled, so she was no longer his enemy.

In a panic he tried to lift her, but his injured arm was still useless. "Oh god oh god."

He began dragging the girl along the ground, toward Alice's hut.

Laricia, daughter of Herbert the Jabberwock Slayer, opened her eyes, thinking she was awakening from her nightly sleep.

Then she grew confused—it was bright and warm here, the middle of the day.

She looked around and saw trees. She was in a forest, lying on a curious substance. She felt with her hands and realized she was lying on leaves.

Then she remembered she'd fought the Jabberwock and lost. She took in a sharp gasp of breath and felt the panic surge within her.

She felt dizzy. She touched her belly and when she pulled her hand away, her fingertips came away coated in blood.

She sat up.

"I should be dead," she muttered to herself. She looked at something lying on the ground.

It was a notepad with a message written upon it—she saw the feather quill pen a short distance away, the tip of it pointing out from the leaves.

She had a hard time reaching the notepad without falling over—she was still tipsy.

She had trouble focusing her eyes—the words were written in blood, she now saw.

Written on the paper were these words: "You fulfilled your duty, for you gave your life defending his honour. Let us not fight anymore."

She grunted in disgust, and looked around for the vorpal sword. Of course the disgusting beast had taken it. She screamed and tore the note in half, then she shouted at the top of her lungs, hoping he was still close enough to hear: "One day, Jabberwock!...I will come for you!"

Her voice echoed throughout the forest.

A short distance away, the Jabberwock heard her—heard that hatred in her voice and stopped in his tracks. He lowered his head, staring at the ground, then continued walking toward his post outside the Eighth Square.

Alice heard the voice of a young girl and raised her head. She stared out the window for a long time, remembering her little sister, who she hadn't last seen alive since she was still a baby.

The Black Butterfly

When Alice was 7

Alice was going about her daily rounds. The next stop was a visit to the Caterpillar.

He liked to sit atop his mushroom with a hookah and smoke various spices. He liked to try numerous and new varieties, which he often tested on Alice first. Sometimes the spices were fun and sometimes they were horrifying or made her sick.

Since the Caterpillar was an ordinary-sized insect, she had to shrink down to his size to interact with him. That's why she carried a piece of his mushroom. It had magical properties so that it could shrink or enlarge Alice.

On that particular day, as she looked down, she could see that the Caterpillar had a visitor—a black butterfly who was resting on the ground in front of him. They seemed to be talking, but as large as Alice was, their voices just sounded like tiny insect murmurs that she couldn't make out.

She nibbled on the mushroom piece, then began to shrink.

She was behind the Caterpillar and he didn't even seem to notice her presence.

The Black Butterfly noticed Alice but didn't acknowledge her. There were a couple of peculiar things about the butterfly. She seemed to be wearing two tiny shoes upon two of her legs—they looked like Mary Janes. And the butterfly seemed to be glowing with a kind of aura...of goody goodiness.

"Ahahah!" said the Black Butterfly. "Look at you, still sitting up there like a grub on a log. Still too afraid to metamorphosize?"

"Quit bullying me! I've already told you I'm not afraid! I just like being a caterpillar."

"No, you're just too scared of growing up! All the other caterpillars from our egg batch have gone on to be butterflies. Except you. What's wrong with you, that your progress is so...delayed? Hmm? Maybe you're too dumb to figure it out."

"I'll transform someday, when I feel like it. What does it matter to you? None of the other butterflies give me a hard time about it."

"Awah. I'm just trying to help you not be such a loser. They all talk behind your back, but I'm the only one nice enough to say it to your face."

"No, you're just a vicious harlot. With wings of black."

"Yes, I definitely stand apart. I'm not ordinary, like all the others." She sneered.

Alice continued watching silently, not knowing what to make of it all. She couldn't understand the goody aura around the butterfly, since she didn't seem so very goody at all. The Caterpillar still hadn't noticed her standing behind him.

"One day," the Caterpillar said, in a whiny voice, "the other butterflies will banish you just like they banished the black rose that transformed you."

She chuckled. "Pish posh. I am more powerful, and much more vicious than any of them will ever be. They are too afraid to ever do anything against me. But even as pathetic as they all are, they are *still* above you, you lowly grub!"

The Caterpillar drew back and whimpered. Alice felt sorry for him, and for a moment thought about stepping in and saying something, but then she thought that might be too humiliating for him. The Black Butterfly winked at her—she seemed to be putting on a cruel show for Alice's benefit.

The Black Butterfly cackled. "Well, I have other things to do than stare at you, pathetic grub. So I just dropped by to hear you say it before I go back to my tree. So are you pathetic?"

The Caterpillar didn't respond.

"Say it! Or I'll beat you up and take whatever stupid spices you're smoking!"

"I'm pathetic," the Caterpillar muttered.

Alice watched on with her eyes brimming with tears of rage. *How dare that Black Butterfly be so mean to my Caterpillar!*

The Black Butterfly cackled loudly then took flight, swooshing through the air and fluttering briefly over the Caterpillar's head, where she stroked against his face with some of her legs.

"Ow! Stop it!" he whined.

"I'll see you later, grub," the Black Butterfly mocked, then flew off. As she passed over, she gave Alice a vicious smile, then she was gone.

"Oh why won't she just leave me alone!?" the Caterpillar called out.

Alice had never seen the Caterpillar like this, so vulnerable. She knew that he could be mean sometimes, but now she had a better understanding as to the reason why. Maybe he only picked on others because he himself had been picked on so much. She felt sorry for him, and she yearned to go to him and comfort him, but still, she thought it might be best to respect his dignity. She didn't want him to feel ashamed.

And so she quietly backed away to a distance where he couldn't see her, then enlarged herself once again.

She was furious. Alice was determined to go have a "discussion" with her. The Black Butterfly needed to learn that it was really mean to pick on others like that! Why, how would she like it if *she* was being picked on?

Alice looked in the direction the butterfly had flown. She was surprised that she could see a glowing kind of trail floating in the air. It was the goody goody energy that she was sensing, she realized, leaving a trail like a scent for a bloodhound. She giggled at that thought.

And so, like a bloodhound on a trail, she followed it, not knowing what would happen when she got there, but she felt like more than a match for a little butterfly. Why, she could rip off her stupid wings if she wanted. But no, that would be mean. It wouldn't solve anything. Maybe she could reason with the Black Butterfly— explain how she had hurt the Caterpillar's feelings…

And so she followed the glowing trail and soon it led her to a tree and a little nook inside the tree.

She knew she should perhaps be more cautious, but she was still absolutely furious at the Butterfly for treating her friend, the Caterpillar, like that—okay, so maybe he wasn't exactly her friend—he was more like her tormentor, but he was *her* tormentor, and she was possessive.

She grabbed a hold of the tree trunk and clasped on, then she ate a bit of the mushroom to shrink herself. She began to shrink in comparison to the tree and scrambled to keep a grip upon the bark. She managed a fair job of it. She stopped shrinking, holding onto the tree just below the nook entrance.

She hooked her hands onto the edge, then kicked up and hooked her foot and pulled herself up and over.

She peered at what was inside.

It was a cozy little abode indeed. The inside reminded Alice of a cave. She saw the Black Butterfly standing in the nook, asleep. Behind her were two most-peculiar objects—they were two human-sized Mary Jane shoes that looked quite enormous compared to the Butterfly. The two shoes glowed with that same "goody" energy Alice had seen before, but the glow was very strong emanating from the shoes, and she deduced that that is perhaps where the "goody" energy had originated from.

She paused for a moment, steeling herself for what she would have to do next, because she wasn't normally a very mean person, but this butterfly had been bullying the Caterpillar. So the Butterfly had to be taught a lesson, and unfortunately that might mean being a little cruel, but it was for a good cause against a mean insect, she told herself, which justified it somewhat.

Her black dress contained many secret pockets capable of holding much more than seemed possible.

She reached into her pocket and crept silently as a cat up to the sleeping Black Butterfly.

She pulled out the little baggy of spice that she had secretly stolen when the Caterpillar wasn't looking. She didn't feel all that bad about stealing it, since the

Caterpillar had judged the spice to be inferior and had essentially thrown it away.

It was the Spice of Paralyzing Terror and Nightmares.

Alice knew firsthand its effects, because the Caterpillar had tested it on her.

Alice stepped up to the dozing Butterfly. She reared back and smacked the insect across the face, hard!

The Black Butterfly startled awake! "What?" her wild, bug eyes, struggled to focus on Alice as she poured the powdered spice into her hand, then she leaned forward and blew a cloud of spice into the bug's face.

The paralysis it caused was instant. It caused all body movements and functions to freeze except for things like blinking, breathing, and curiously, talking.

If the same thing happened as happened to Alice herself, the waking nightmares would soon be coming on. That was what had happened to Alice the three times the Caterpillar had tested it on her. It had been torturous, but informative.

The Black Butterfly was twerking her mouth, testing her ability to move it. "You! You were standing behind the Caterpillar! His guinea pig," she said with a sneer.

Alice clucked. "Maybe I am, but the thing is, the Caterpillar may be a bit mean at times, but he is *my* Caterpillar, and I don't appreciate insects who mistreat him." She glared.

The Black Butterfly eerily screamed in terror—it was eery because only her mouth moved.

Alice assumed that the Butterfly had begun hallucinating.

It was Alice's plan to terrorize her into never bullying the Caterpillar again.

But first, she was curious. By her estimation, the drug would last ten minutes, so she still had some time. She gestured with her chin to behind the Butterfly.

"What are those shoes?" Alice asked.

"Bug off." She sneered.

Alice stuck her fingers to the edges of her mouth and pulled her mouth wide while making glicky noises with her flapping tongue and rolling her eyes about.

The Butterfly shrieked. "You're a demon!"

Alice could only imagine what she was hallucinating, but it must've been horrific.

"Grrr," Alice said through her stretched mouth. "I am the demon spawn from hell, here to avenge the girl you stole the shoes from."

The Butterfly was blubbering. "*I* didn't steal them. Her stepsisters did."

"Whose stepsisters?"

"You don't know?"

"Tell me, or I'll make the face again!"

"Ack! Okay, they're Cinderella's shoes. Before she got the slippers, she wore the goody two-shoes, but she left them behind. Her stepsisters hid them away in this tree, because they hated her. I would've done the same."

Alice peered at those shoes, wondering why they seemed to glow with a magical aura that had apparently transferred to the Butterfly.

Alice said, "And what magic do these goody-shoes possess?"

"What are you, dense? Everybody knows what goody two-shoes do. They make the one wearing them follow the rules and perform good deeds and always do the right thing, and bleh, they're quite disgusting, really."

"Then what do you want with them?" She sneered. "Are you guarding them?"

"I wish I could quit them, but ever since I discovered them here in this tree, it's like I'm addicted to them. I long to wear them, even though they are quite oversized and I don't really want to be a goody-goody girl. I guess I'm lucky I can't actually wear them, but I...I like to rub up against them."

"Ah, so that would explain why you wear those *ridiculous* little insect shoes that you do."

"Don't mock me. I think they're cute."

"But you know what's *not* cute?!" She got up in the Black Butterfly's face. "Bullying my friend!" Alice performed a trick she had learned wherein she rolled her eyeballs upwards so that her eyes seemed to have turned completely white.

The Butterfly shrieked, but then she protested, "But he's a loser. He's afraid to grow up."

"That is not your concern!" She thumped the Butterfly hard in the forehead with a flick of her finger.

"Ow! That hurt!"

Alice wanted to use the hallucinations to bring up terror in the Butterfly's mind whenever she even *thought* of bullying the Caterpillar. "Listen up, you wench! From now on, you're gonna leave the Caterpillar alone, got it? For I am a demon, I am Satan incarnate, I shall hunt you down and defile you!" Alice didn't actually understand what any of those words meant, but she'd read a story once where they were used to great effect.

"But he's a loser," she muttered, her voice trembling with fright.

"I don't care! He's my friend! And from now on, you stay far away from him! You don't speak to him, you don't look at him, you got it?!"

"Okay, okay," she whimpered.

"And if you do, I'll cut you…and…I'll tear your soul apart!" She made guttural demonic noises while sticking two fingers up behind her head like devil's horns. "Blehhhhahaha I am a demon from hell… Leave him alone! Got it?!"

"Ye-yes… I shall never even talk to him again! Please don't tear my soul apart," she whimpered.

Alice knew the spice would be wearing off soon. She looked longingly at the Mary Janes behind the Black Butterfly. "Do you mind if I take the goody two-shoes? They don't fit you anyway."

"Mind? Heck no! Please take them! They have a hold on me, a magical hold, that causes me to obsess over them! Oh, it shall be a good day if you take them away. Let their goody goody power infest *you*."

Alice arched a brow. "You don't like goody goodiness?"

"Absolutely not. So if you want them, please take them."

"Thank you. I shall."

It was a bit tricky getting the shoes out of the tree nook. She had to nibble just a tiny bit of mushroom to grow a little bit so she could pick the shoes up and toss them out to the ground below. She scurried out of the nook, then nibbled some more to grow even larger, then climbed down the tree.

The shoes were adult-sized, whereas she was only 7, so she used a little trick to make the shoes fit—she nibbled enough mushroom to make herself slightly large than usual, so the shoes would fit, then she put them on and shrunk herself to normal sized again. The shoes shrunk along with her.

Voila! Now she had two goody two-shoes to wear.

She looked forward to following rules and being a right and proper little girl who always did the appropriate thing. The shoes glowed bright for a while then their glow disappeared, but she could still feel their magical goody energy going up her through her toesies.

She caught the Black Butterfly cautiously peeking out the nook. Alice scowled and used two fingers to point at her own eyes, then the Butterfly's.

She left her old shoes behind, then in order to break in her new goody two-shoes, she skipped all the way to the Caterpillar's mushroom.

"You're late!" boomed the Caterpillar after she had shrunk down to his size.

She couldn't stop smiling. "I'm sorry. I had a matter to attend to."

"What are you grinning about?"

Alice began climbing up the mushroom.

The Caterpillar said, "I've got a bunch of new spices I'd like to try on you."

Alice was next to him now. She admired the scowl on his face. This was *her* Caterpillar, and he wouldn't be bullied anymore.

"Why are you looking at me like that, silly girl?"

"I'm just glad that you're you!" She wrapped her arms around him and planted a big kiss on his cheek.

He squirmed. "Ugh! Get off of me! We've got to test these spices."

So Alice let go of him and stared at him with a big dopey grin until he asked her to stop.

THE RED QUEEN

When Alice was 10

The Red Queen hovered in the air inside the small dungeon room. As usual, her legs were racing back and forth as she ran, but she remained in the same place. She'd supposedly been "captured" by the Tweedle twins, but the fact of the matter was that she herself had called out to them, asking them to take her to the Queen of Heart's dungeons.

The Queen of Hearts was about to visit, she'd been told. There was a knock upon the iron door, then the Queen of Heart's voice announcing her own presence: "Her Highness is coming in." The door opened and there was the Queen of Hearts, with an unreadable expression upon her face.

The Red Queen called, "Welcome, Your Highness, to my humble abode. I'm afraid I can't speak long, as I've got to go somewhere." Then suddenly remembering, the Red Queen said, "Sorry, force of habit."

"Yes," said the Queen of Hearts as she stepped into the room. She left the door open. There were guard cards stationed outside. But the Red Queen had little to fear, because after all, she had *chosen* to be imprisoned.

The Queen of Hearts looked pointedly at the stone walls of the small cell. "I daresay, if you get to going where your legs seem to want, you shall run right smack into that wall."

"True. Even so, I quite enjoy focusing upon my running, despite what folly it might seem to you."

The Queen of Hearts said, "Well I thought it would be remiss of me not to at least welcome you to my dungeon. I know we have not always been on the best of terms."

"Yes. We were mortal enemies, but those days are no longer. Now I wish solely to focus upon my running. You may go about the business of *your* running, running the kingdom that is."

A wicked grin formed on the Queen of Heart's face. "So you relinquish your crown?"

"I concede to your authority. You may go ahead and be the Queen of all of Wonderland. It's all quite a bother, anyway."

The Queen of Hearts scowled. "That's it? How anticlimactic."

"Well I don't wish to fight you, if that's what you mean. No, I'm perfectly content to stay here in your dungeon. In fact, it will be good for me. I daresay I much prefer it."

The Queen of Hearts huffed in frustration. "We have a long rivalry, you and I, so I can't pretend I'm not disappointed that I won't get to behead you. You know, I know it's not your fault, but I've grown *quite* irritated over the years over the fact that some citizens of Wonderland have come to think of you and I as the same person!"

The Red Queen chuckled politely, while still running. Always running. "Yes, it is quite irritating." She laughed at a thought in her head.

"What is it?" said the Queen of Hearts.

"It's just that once I heard of someone asking, 'have you ever seen them in the same room together?' And now here we are, finally, in the same room."

"But no one can see."

The Red Queen said, "So perhaps the rumors shall persist."

"Perhaps," agreed the Queen of Hearts. "But I don't see how they could confuse us. After all, *I* am not the one who continually runs in place. I've always wondered why you do that. Don't you know you'll get places faster, if you actually move forward?"

"Of course I know that," the Red Queen snapped. "You just don't know where I'm coming from."

"Where you're coming from?! My dear, you're always in the same place!"

"It hasn't always been thus. You don't know my situation."

The Queen of Hearts smirked. "Should I run a mile in your shoes then?" She laughed a little at the pout that formed upon the Red Queen's face. "Oh, don't be such a priss. Why don't you just tell me, then?"

"You wouldn't understand."

"I shan't leave until you tell me."

The Red Queen sighed. "Very well! I have had much time to think about things, and the inner workings of my own mind and my reasons. I'll tell you succinctly: I am running from the past."

"The past? Is it so terrible?"

The Red Queen said, "Yes, for I betrayed the man I loved."

The Queen of Hearts laughed. "The man you loved? You mean that little pawn you had a fling with?"

"No, that was a grave mistake on my part. The man I loved is my husband and I might someday break his heart because I cheated on him."

Another chuckle from the Queen of Hearts. "*Someday?* You mean it hasn't happened yet?"

"No, because he is currently sleeping, but I felt that if I ran fast enough, perhaps it all might not catch up with him, and me."

The Queen of Hearts laughed. "All of that drama over a silly little pawn! My dear, they are your playthings!

You shouldn't be ashamed to use them however you desire."

The Red Queen shook her head. "No. They don't deserve that sort of treatment. You forget, I was a pawn once, before the Red King came to love me."

Another laugh. "That's pathetic! You should be ashamed of the fact you were once a pawn, yes, but embrace your future, where *you* use the pawns! That's what I'd do! Even better now that he's asleep! When the cat sleeps, the mice play!"

The Red Queen sighed. "You just don't understand love. Perhaps no one has ever loved you."

The Queen of Hearts scowled. "Watch yourself. I have been nice by allowing you this cell. I could have you beheaded."

"Well I *have* known love, by the most honourable, respectful man in Wonderland. But I threw it all away for a meaningless tryst. The shock of it threw him into a sleep from which he has not awakened all these years. In fact, I am afraid of what would happen if he does. Perhaps I am merely his own dream, and I shall disappear entirely, or perhaps the past shall finally catch up with me…" She sighed forlornly.

"Well, forget the past then, I say. What's wrong with the future?"

"I don't want a future that doesn't include him."

"Crikey, you're pathetic! I tell you what, I shall rouse him…"

"No! I just want to run here, in my own private purgatory. Perhaps, in this way, he still loves me."

"You never seem to get anywhere. Why is that?"

"I don't know."

The Queen of Hearts scowled. "You shall tell me, or I shan't leave."

The Red Queen sighed. "Very well. Much as I hate to admit it to myself, the future frightens me, just as the past does, so I run just enough to stay in the same place. Oh, but I try to not even admit that to myself. Much better to fool myself into thinking I want to go somewhere."

"I see," said the Queen of Hearts, considering her, rubbing her chin as if the Red Queen were an intriguing specimen.

"Are you happy now?! Can I be left alone to run in peace?"

The Queen of Hearts held up her finger. "Well, I shall certainly leave you alone in this dungeon."

She sighed in relief. "Thanks."

"But there is just one last thing."

"Yes?"

"It's just that the guards have informed me that they have overheard you reciting a poem to yourself from time to time. Do you know of what I speak?"

The Red Queen swallowed. "Yes."

"Could you recite it to me? Then I promise that I shall leave you to your…running."

"Promise?"

"Yes. After all, I've grown quite bored with you actually. Just this one more thing…"

"Very well.

And the Red Queen recited her poem that she would normally only recite to herself, when she was alone:

Sometimes, you wish out loud to scream,
To awaken yourself from someone else's dream,
Where the way that you are isn't the way that you seem.

But then, the man who loved you might no longer care,
So you keep your past behind you, to keep him unaware,
And run and run away from it, while going *to* nowhere.

To let his dream of you go unharassed,
You mustn't reach a future, and you cannot face the past,
For if right now's forever, his love will always last.

After the Queen of Hearts heard the poem, her face turned pale. She nodded, then turned and exited the room.

The door slammed shut behind her.

BLaCK RoSe

When Alice was 7

The encounter with the Black Butterfly had inspired Alice. She'd inquired discreetly about the Black Rose, then waited until the right opportunity presented itself. When it did, she marched in her magic goody two-shoes up to the Garden of Live Flowers.

It was a flower-bed of talking flowers who seemed to think that Alice herself was a flower. Alice had never corrected them of the notion, because she quite enjoyed the feeling of fitting in.

She always had to talk first. "Wake up, flowers!"

The Tiger-lily said, "Greetings flower Alice."

Alice enjoyed their company, but only in small doses, since they had certain notions that would grate on her nerves. For one thing, they thought she wasn't colorful enough, because she always wore a black dress (which they considered her petals). She cut right to the chase. "I've heard tell that there was once a black rose who inhabited your garden. Can you tell me any more about her?"

The Tiger-lily gasped. "The Black Rose?!"

And here all the other flowers gasped (though they did not breath like people did) then they grew silent, which was puzzling, because they'd always been a bunch of chatterboxes.

"That's right," Alice said. "What's wrong?"

"Where did you hear of the Black Rose?!" the Tiger-lily demanded.

"I've been asking around. There was a butterfly who was said to feast upon its nectar in order to turn black..."

"Yes, there was a rose who let blackness overtake her, and she was banished from the garden."

Alice felt sorrow rise up within her. She thought that a black rose might actually be quite pretty. Perhaps the Black Rose was simply a misunderstood outcast much like Alice herself. Maybe the Black Rose could use a friend to help her. "Where was she banished to?"

"Well, before we speak any further, you shall remove those wretched shoes. We despise them."

"What do you mean?"

"The shoes..."

Alice tended to be most agreeable, so she removed her shoes. "Now please tell me more."

"Figure it out yourself."

Alice completely lost her temper. With an outraged shriek, she reached out and grasped the Tiger-lily's stem. "Tell me, or I shall begin plucking your petals!"

The other flowers gasped. One yelled, "Let her go!" The Tiger-lily said, "You wouldn't dare." But Alice could feel that the flower was trembling ever-so-slightly, as much as a plant could reasonably be expected to, at least.

Alice reached out and pulled a petal off. "He loves me..."

The Tiger-lily shrieked in pain.

Alice dropped the petal then reached out, touched another one. "He loves me not..."

"Stop! I'll tell you! For the love of god, stop!"

And that was how Alice learned where the Black Rose had been relocated to by a mysterious cloaked flower tender they had summoned. Alice felt bad about being so cruel to get her way. She was usually such a good girl, but sometimes she just snapped, and they *had* made her take off her goody two-shoes, after all. Awkwardly, she left the garden, not wanting to make a bad situation worse. She'd have to make it up to the flowers somehow later.

They'd told her there was a stone archway set in the side of a hill a short distance away. Soon she saw it, tucked away discreetly in the middle of a forest. They said to look for a button on the archway to press to open the door.

She looked upon the edges of the gray-stoned archway. It was lined with carved runes that she couldn't read. Then she saw the button, but it seemed to be at the height of an adult. She was just a little girl, and she almost couldn't reach it. She had to stand on her tippy-toes and stretch. "Errrgh." Then she struggled to press the button in hard enough, but, then "Ahah!" she exclaimed as she pressed it in.

A blade of metal suddenly slid out above Alice. She could see that it was at just the right height to have decapitated any adult who pressed the button. She had been spared death on account of being short. She wondered if maybe she should turn back.

After a few seconds, the blade retracted, then the door slid upward.

She peered inside to see a square medium-sized room cut from gray stone.

In the middle of the room was a skeleton wearing a royal gown and crown sitting in a golden throne. Next to the throne was a pedestal atop of which rested a black rose within a flower pot. A glass dome rested over the flower and a note was attached to the inner surface of the dome, with hand written words upon it, but she couldn't read the note from her distance.

Alice briefly considered turning back, because this might be a rather precarious situation. But then she thought maybe the Black Rose was extremely lonely, and her heart filled with such sorrow for the rose's possible distress.

"Black Rose!" she called out. "Can you hear me?"

She thought she heard the flower give a muffled cry, but she couldn't make out the words through the glass.

"Fear not!" she proclaimed, "For I am here to rescue you from your predicament!" She stepped through the door then rolled on the ground into a crouch where she listened intently and peered around for any threat.

The door slammed shut behind her and she gasped and looked around. She was trapped.

"Oh bother," she muttered to herself.

Then she heard a kind of gurgling sound. Clear liquid began trickling from the edges of the room from little round holes. With dread, Alice assumed it was acid, because of course it would be!

The only way to avoid the acid was to stand atop the throne, so she performed three expert cartwheels toward it, then hopped atop the arms of the throne, balancing precariously. She didn't want to touch the icky skeleton.

The clear liquid reached the bottom of the throne and the fabric of the gown. A hissing bubbling sound issued forth as the acid began to dissolve cloth and bone and a pungent smoke rose up.

"Oh, this will not do!" Alice proclaimed, feeling sorry for herself. The acid level was slowly rising.

"Oh, what should I do, Black Rose?"

Again, the Black Rose seemed to speak, but again, she couldn't make out the words.

Alice hugged herself in terror, as the liquid of burning death approached. She looked around. There was nowhere else to stand. The ceiling was lined with rows of round holes and a larger hole above the Black Rose, but the ceiling was twenty feet above her, so she couldn't reach them.

While trembling with fear, she watched the level of acid rise, burning the skeleton and its dress, leaving the throne untouched, perhaps because it was made of gold, she thought.

"Help! Won't someone please help?!"

But there was no response. And then her tears began to flow. She flicked them from her face in frustration. The acid continued to rise, but now, the sizzling and smoke seemed to lessen.

My tears! A few of them dropped in the acid! Perhaps their magic negates it.

So she leaned forward and allowed as many of her tears to drip down into the acid as she could. Soon the sizzling and dissolving stopped and Alice laughed out loud in relief. The level of the liquid continued to rise though, and soon it rose over the throne and Alice could no longer avoid being immersed.

Soon she was drenched in it and had to tread water to stay afloat in the former acid. She suspected the liquid had been transformed into tears.

It continued rising.

I shall drown in my own tears, she thought morosely.

But then thankfully, the liquid began to drain from the room. While it was doing so, and Alice was busy treading in place, she took the time to read the note on the inside of the (apparently waterproof) glass dome over the flower. It read: "Smell me."

"Black Rose, can you hear me? I need you to just hold on for me, okay? We're gonna get you out."

The Black Rose shook a little. It seemed kind of like a nod, Alice thought.

The liquid had all drained. "Well, then. Now that that's done with, let's smell what all the fuss is about, shall we?"

That's when she heard a loud clamor of clanks from the ceiling. She looked up to see rows of steel spikes burst from the holes in the ceiling, then a creaking sound issued forth as the ceiling began lowering!

Panic came over Alice. Frantically, her mind searched for a way out of this predicament.

The mushroom!

She carried a piece of the Caterpillar's mushroom, so that she would be able to shrink down to his size whenever she needed to visit him. She reached into one of the inner pockets of her sopping dress, and pulled out the piece of mushroom. It was regrettably soggy, but now was not the time to be finicky, was it?

She nibbled and began shrinking, with the descending spikes following closely behind. She hoped she would be able to shrink fast enough. The ceiling was crushing the throne, the black rose's dome safely slipped into a hole in the ceiling, and Alice kept shrinking.

She reassured herself that there were no holes in the ground that would allow the spikes to slide in, so there would be space next to the spikes…

That was her only hope—to stand in one of the spaces between the spikes to avoid being skewered.

She looked up to the ceiling. The spikes had completely crushed the throne and the tips had almost reached the ground. She took a step to the side as the spikes clanked into the ground all around her.

She breathed a sigh of relief.

Then a dreadful, long moment passed.

Then a clanking sound as of chains being retracted, and creaking noises as the ceiling rose back up to its original position. The spikes retracted.

"Crikey, but that was close!" she yelled. She nibbled some mushroom to grow again.

She walked up to the pedestal. It was a bit tall for her, so she nibbled a little extra mushroom.

"Finally! Now I know from fairy tales that these things go in threes. Since I survived the three challenges, there shan't be any more." And with that proclamation, she lifted the glass dome off the Black Rose. "Black Rose, can you speak?"

Not all flowers could speak, and not all flowers that could speak spoke alike, and the words came from the flower as a whispery hiss. "Smelll meeeee."

Alice shrugged. "As you wish. You are a most beautiful flower. I'm sure your scent is just as much so."

She leaned over and inhaled.

And was transported—into a world unknown to her. Darkness and naughtiness and adult secrets swirled about. She experienced the delicious dessert of revenge served unexpected, and the malicious candy of destroying what others cherished. She felt and smelled the allure of seduction employed solely to betray. The corruption of innocence was this flower's scent. These were the shadows of unadmitted desires and sensations. She shuddered with the delicious chill.

She could feel the power of her goody two-shoes negating the corrupting influence, and debated whether to take them off.

But then she swooned and fell to the floor, lost in an unblinking daze. She was conscious, but unable to move.

She was unaware of how much time passed—it could have been seconds, it could have been centuries, when she felt someone or something grab a hold of her arms and drag her out of the room to the forest outside.

She was unable to blink and her eyes stung as they stared into the clouds above.

She saw a cloaked arm pass over, holding a glass tube, then something was held beneath her nose. She smelled the aroma of a pungent chemical. She instantly jolted and was able to move again.

She shifted her eyes to see a mysterious hooded cloaked figure holding the Black Rose in its pot.

Alice said, "Who are you? What happened?"

Alice could only see the glowing twinkle of two red eyes beneath the hood. "Shhh." The mysterious being lifted a bony gray finger to its mouth. "Your kind is not yet ready for the beauty of the Black Rose."

"You mean humans?"

"No, I mean little girls."

"I'm not so little. I'm almost 8."

"Yes…little girl. You went too far from home, young one."

Alice got the sense that it was speaking figuratively. "I just wanted to help. I'm sorry."

"One day perhaps, you will be ready. But this is not the day. Go back to your former life now. I am putting the Black Rose in a different place, to await those who are ready. As for this place…" It pointed to the stone doorway. "It will explode in ten seconds. I suggest you run."

When Alice shifted her eyes from the doorway back to the figure, it was suddenly gone and she couldn't be entirely sure it had even ever been there in the first place. Then her eyes went wide in alarm as she hurried to stand and run as fast as she could away from the doomed place.

The sound of a huge explosion erupted behind her then heat licked at her back and threw her ten feet through the air. Her head landed just a few inches from the trunk of a tree. Debris and ash rained down upon her from the sky.

She realized her blond hair was on fire and shrieked and rolled about to put out the flame—she hoped her hair hadn't been blackened.

Then she dusted herself off and returned to her hut. She snuck back into her chains. The guard card was still taking a nap.

When he awoke, he seemed puzzled by Alice's singed hair and the burn holes in her dress, but the guard card wasn't very bright, so the matter was quickly forgotten by him.

As she sat there, her thoughts were quite different than usual. She ruminated upon the delectable pleasures of torture. She wondered at the allure of licking the tears of others' pain and humiliation. And she thought, uncharacteristically for her, of how delicious revenge must be.

How great it must be to thoroughly vanquish and humiliate one's enemies? To plant death's kiss upon their cheeks, while raining your unrelenting revenge upon them? And upon their graves, to place…a single black rose…

BIRTHDay PaRTY

When Alice was 8

Calloo Callay! What a frabjuous day!

It was a splendid day, indeed, for today was Alice's 8th birthday!

In the short time she'd been here, the citizens of Wonderland had grown so fond of using the girl for the sake of their own pleasure, and today was their chance to celebrate that!

Everybody who was anybody was gathered in the Queen of Heart's ballroom, which was filled with the dancing revelers and an assortment of cakes, snacks and foods. There was even a table of tarts that only the Queen was allowed to eat (heavily guarded of course, to prevent any further thefts).

"Welcome!" the Queen called out to the crowd of assembled revelers, as she held a glass of sparkling apple juice. "I'm so glad you all could attend." She gazed out at the crowd, searching. She saw the Tweedles, Humpty Dumpty, the Mad Hatter, March Hare, Dormouse, even the Jabberwock was there, looking awkward and shy. And there even was the grinning floating head of the Cheshire Cat, whom she hadn't even invited. "Now, we just have to wait for the birthday girl herself to get here!"

That brought up a round of polite laughter from the crowd.

The Queen said, "But I'm sure she'll be along shortly. So, eat, be merry and dance, and when she gets here, the party shall truly begin and we shall unleash all our planned festivities!"

That brought a cheer, and the Queen left the crowd to it and began mingling.

Meanwhile, Alice sat at her desk she was chained to, inside her humble, sparse hut. Today was her 8th birthday, but since she was stuck in this horrendous, stifling world, she didn't expect anyone to throw her a party, and just as she'd expected, no one had invited her to one. She sighed and pouted miserably. She supposed there was always the possibility that they would throw her a surprise party, just like they surprised her with unhappy unbirthday parties every day. And the day wasn't over, so she still held out hope.

So Alice was now spending her birthday at her desk, drawing upon a sheet of paper. She was drawing a picture of a girl who was chained to a desk. There was a huge cake in front of the drawn girl and she was holding her hand out toward it, but the chain wasn't long enough to reach. There was a big frown upon the girl's face. Alice felt like she wanted to draw tears, but that might be a difficult thing to draw.

The guard card who watched over her was no good company at all. He was seated in his chair, dozing.

She heard the sound of the door opening and grinned. *Here comes my surprise birthday party! Oh, this just has to be it!*

But when the door swung open, there before her eyes, was a girl she couldn't recall ever having seen before.

The girl was wearing a white lace veil over her face. She looked to be a teenager, wearing a long, fluffy black dress much like Alice's own. There were splotches of what looked like dried blood splattering her dress. The girl's right hand donned a black metal gauntlet like from a suit of armor, adorned with ornamental engravings and an odd, repeating symbol. She held a box with a handle atop it in her other hand.

Alice gasped and called out to the guard.

"Eh?" the guard said as he lazily opened his eyes. He saw the older girl and began to stand, as the girl calmly walked up to him and punched him so hard he knocked back into the chair and toppled backward into it with a crash. He lay unconscious upon the ground.

"Oh no!" Alice cried.

The girl was kneeling. She took the gauntlet off, then began rummaging through the metal box. "Don't worry," she said. "I won't harm you. I'm here to warn you."

At the Queen of Heart's ballroom, Humpty Dumpty was throwing a hissy fit. "Where is Alice!? I have a bucket of paint I had prepared especially to pour over her head!"

"Yes," said Tweedledum. "It's quite rude for her to show up late for her own birthday party!" "Yes, quite!" said Tweedledee. They crossed their arms.

"Yes," added the March Hare. "Doesn't she know how to tell time? She knows what time the party starts correct?" He was peering at the large oversized clock he wore around his neck.

The Queen of Hearts tried to control her irritation. "Yes, of course she does. It was right on her invitation, just like with all of yours."

"Well, then it's quite inconsiderate of her," said the March Hare.

The Queen of Hearts said, "Well, she's still not *too* late. Perhaps she'll be along shortly. But in the meantime, let's have some of her cake, shall we?"

"Warn me of what?" asked Alice. She watched as the veiled girl brought out two handcuffs from her metal box and put them on the card's wrists.

"I am from the future," said the girl. She began putting the other pair of cuffs around the guard card's ankles. She stood, kicked the card's spear away, then looked at Alice, said, "I am here to warn you not to let your heart grow black."

Alice chuckled at the very idea. "Well of course I won't, but why exactly did you want to tell me that?"

The girl sighed. "Listen. You're still new here. But I know…from personal experience. This place, the creatures and people here can be very cruel, and over time, it can, I mean it *will* really tear you down, make you start thinking negative thoughts. You might start thinking about getting revenge, hurting those who hurt you…"

Alice giggled. "Oh, that's silly! You can only get negative thoughts if you allow yourself to. That won't happen to me, because I always stay positive."

"I'm sorry, but all their cruelty, over time, it can get to anyone. It happened to me."

Alice frowned. "Well did you think positive thoughts?"

"I did for a long time, until I didn't."

She frowned more. "But did you look on the bright side?"

"I did, but then after all those years, the bright side disappeared, and it became *all* dark side."

Her smile wavered a bit, then reasserted itself. "But did you tell yourself everything was going to be okay?"

"Yes, I did everything you do, but still, over time, I let my heart grow black. And now I regret it."

Alice's mouth was twerking as she thought. "Well if you did all that, then I don't know how you could possibly let your heart grow black. You must have done something wrong. Did you try turning your frown upside down?"

"Yes, but after so many years of people being mean to me, the dark side took me by surprise. That's why I came here. I want to tell you, that over time, all the ways you keep the dark thoughts away might not be enough. Don't always assume you can keep away the darkness on your own."

Alice frowned, but then smiled. "Aww, don't worry. Everything will be okay."

"No! Listen to me! Things might not all be okay! They could turn out very very bad! I was once like you! I didn't take the darkness seriously, and now…" She pointed at the splotches of reddish-brown on her dress. "This is the blood of boys whose hearts I ripped out after causing them to love me."

Alice frowned, but this time her smile did not reappear. "That sounds mean."

"It *was* mean! Because I let my heart grow black! Listen, you must promise me, to do whatever you can. You must *fight* it, don't you understand? You must fight the darkness! Never let your guard down!"

Alice nodded and her lower lip began to tremble. She felt like she was going to cry, because this lady was scaring her.

The girl said, "Good. I've got your attention. I know the citizens of Wonderland can be cruel, but never let their cruelty rub off on you. Never give in to hatred, never let them get you down."

In a whisper, Alice said, "I won't. They just don't know any better. I will teach them to be kind."

The girl laughed sadly. "Just promise me you'll never let your heart grow black. You gotta do whatever it takes."

Alice's eyes went wide. "I promise. And those guys don't get to me. The meaner they get, the *nicer* I get! I'll kill them with kindness!"

Again the girl laughed sadly. "That's the spirit. I wish I could do more than just warn you, like provide you magic protection or something, but all I can do is use my own words and experience."

"Aw, don't feel bad," said Alice.

The girl softly shook her head. Meanwhile the guard card was regaining consciousness and slowly figuring out his condition.

The girl said, "Now I know it's your birthday, because I had to wait till today to speak to you, because of how the timelines interact, so I brought you this." She reached into her iron box and pulled out a chocolate cupcake with a candle stuck in the top.

"Ooh, is that for me?" said Alice. "I thought everyone had forgotten my birthday."

"I could never forget," said the girl just before she struck a match and lit the candle.

The guard card struggled and shouted, "Who are you? Let me out!"

Alice watched as the girl set the birthday cupcake upon her desk, and then Alice lost control and burst into tears. "Thank you so much!"

"You're welcome sweetie." She set two keys next to the cupcake.

"Halt! Surrender yourself!" called the guard card.

"Blow out your candle," said the girl gently.

Alice closed her eyes, made her wish, then blew out the candle. She expected it to go out, but then relight, just like the candles the citizens of Wonderland tormented her with during her unhappy unbirthday parties.

But when she opened her eyes again, the candle was extinguished and unleashing gray smoke.

The girl was walking away.

"It's your birthday?" said the guard card. He sounded remorseful.

"Where are you going?" said Alice.

The girl's voice sounded choked up. "I'm sorry. I can't stay." She picked up her things, put the gauntlet back on. "Happy birthday." She began walking toward the door.

"Lady?" Alice said.

She turned her head to look backward. "Yes?"

"I'm real sorry your heart turned black."

"Thank you," and as she turned away, Alice thought she could see tears brimming in her eyes.

And then the mysterious veiled woman was gone.

In the ballroom, all of Alice's birthday cake had been eaten. A near riot was on the Queen of Heart's hands because of the crowd's outrage. Numerous humiliations and indignities of Alice had been planned for her party, and now with her nonarrival, those plans were ruined.

Alice was now extremely late, and it seemed likely that the devious urchin was *intentionally* choosing not to show up.

The Queen of Hearts had put on a smiling face earlier, but now she could no longer hide her rage. She was supremely offended. "How dare she ignore my invitation!" she said to no one in particular. "I even went out of my way to make her a very special card, quite separate from all the ordinary unexciting kind I gave to all the other little people."

Next to her, Humpty Dumpty huffed. "Well, I never." He crossed his stubby arms and turned away from her.

The Queen felt the need to defend herself. "Well, her card *was* special. Not boring like the kind for the plebeians like you! I went through a lot of trouble making that card!"

Humpty huffed louder and turn away even further.

The Queen once again felt the need to defend herself. "Well, I did! It was lined with real gold and covered in purple glitter, in the shape of a heart. I had my court's best calligrapher write the note upon it with all sorts of swirly doodads."

"Like this?" said the March Hare.

The Queen turned to see that he was holding Alice's invitation card in his hand. He explained, "It was setting atop a table next to some escargot."

The Queen snapped her fingers. "Ooh! Now I remember setting the card there. Why, I must have forgotten to send the card off…but errr," in a loud voice she proclaimed, "But I did it on purpose, for if a girl can't be bothered to inquire about and find out when her *own* birthday party is, then she doesn't deserve to attend hers at *all*. So, Her Majesty doth declare she is greatly offended by this *Alice's* non-attendance, and for this offense, Her Majesty declares that Alice shan't be allowed to any more of her birthday parties!"

"Hear hear!" the call rose up from the crowd.

Of the two keys the mysterious veiled girl had left upon Alice's desk, one was the key to her own chains, which the guard card usually carried. The other key turned out to be for the handcuffs bounding the guard card.

The guard card was quite distraught after Alice unlocked him.

He whimpered, "If the Queen of Hearts finds out I was sleeping on my post, she'll have me beheaded for sure!"

He sounded so miserable that Alice took pity on him. "Don't worry. I shan't tell."

"Oh thank you, thank you!"

"Yes," Alice said, as she used the key to rechain herself to her desk. "As a matter of fact, let's not mention anything about this incident to anyone, shall we?"

"Oh, absolutely not. It shall be our little secret."

Alice tossed the key to the guard. "I only ask one thing of you…"

"Yes, what, Miss Alice?"

"Eat half of my birthday cupcake? It's lonely to celebrate one's birthday alone. Everyone else seems to have forgotten."

"Certainly, Miss Alice. It's the least I can do."

The crowd was gathered outside the Queen of Heart's ballroom. In front of them was a scarecrow that someone had placed a blond wig on.

The Queen of Hearts stood beside the scarecrow as the crowd shouted, "Burn the witch! Burn the witch!"

The Queen of Hearts was holding a blazing torch. "That's right!" she called out to the crowd. "This is what we think of stuck up girls who are so conceited that they can't even show up to their *own* birthday party! But we are no longer gonna put up with little stuck up Alice anymore! This is what we do to girls like you!" She pressed the torch to the mannequin and it caught aflame. "We burn you in effigy! Damn you, Alice! Damn you straight to hell!"

Stolen Tarts

When Alice was 7 (before she arrived in Wonderland)

The Queen of Hearts was walking through the hallway feeling quite puzzled and annoyed. She'd gotten a message about an "urgent matter" but when she'd rushed to the throne room, no one seemed to know who sent the message or what it was about, so the Queen decided to go back to her ballroom.

"Someone's head shall roll for this screw up, that's for certain," she muttered to herself. She had been *quite* enjoying herself before she had been called away. This distraction was the *second* thing that had gone wrong with the party so far—the other thing was that the Jabberwock had misread his invitation and showed up an hour early, then left before the ball even began!

It was a masquerade ball and she was wearing a mask. Of course, everyone knew it was her, due to her elaborate dress. No one was allowed to have a better dress than her, after all. The only dress splendid enough to be comparable to this one was…the original version of this dress. She'd unfortunately torn it along the sleeve and so she'd had a duplicate made, which she was wearing now.

Come to think of that torn dress, she'd seemed to have misplaced it earlier this morning, but what did it matter, really.

She was approaching the doors to the ballroom, besides which stood two frog guards wearing powdered wigs.

"Welcome back, Your Majesty," said one of them.

"Shush!" she said. "I'm supposed to be in disguise, remember?"

"Of course My Queen."

That's when the door suddenly flung open to reveal someone wearing the Queen's duplicate dress running out of the ballroom. Since the person wore a mask, it was impossible to tell who it was.

Behind the person came the yell, "Stop! Thief!"

The person was looking behind him or herself as they ran, not looking where they were going. They turned their head forward just in time for the Queen of Hearts to land a solid punch across the person's face, knocking him or her flat on their back and seemingly unconscious.

One of the guard cards ran up to the prone person and pointed a spear at him/her.

The Queen said, "What is going on here?"

The card said, "That impostor stole Your Highness's tarts!"

Other guards arrived on the scene and handcuffed the thief. Behind them, the crowd of partygoers watched, whilst whispering amongst themselves.

"Who is it!?" demanded the Queen.

A guard lowered the mask to reveal that it was the Knave of Hearts! He began to come to.

She said, "Did he eat any of my tarts? Guard, check his breath!"

A guard squeezed the Knave's cheeks and sniffed his breath. "I don't smell any tarts, Your Highness."

"Thank goodness! Search him!"

Now the Knave spoke. "I didn't steal the tarts. They were already gone when I lifted the lid!"

As the guards searched him, the Queen furiously said, "Are you telling me that your defense is that you *tried* to steal my tarts, but someone else beat you to it?"

"Yes Your Highness. It is the truth!"

The guard cards had found no tarts. "They're not here, Your Highness."

She had been looking forward to eating those delectable tarts in front of the crowd while everyone watched with envy. She'd set the tarts upon a table in the middle of the ballroom beneath a metal dome with a sign next to it that read: "These tarts are the Queen of

Heart's and you shan't have none, or ye shall be executed." The fact that they'd been stolen was a tragedy. With overwhelming sadness, the Queen looked to the guard. "Are my tarts truly gone? All of them?"

"I'm afraid so, Your Highness."

She turned red with fury and pointed at the Knave. "Off with his head!"

"But I didn't take them!" the Knave said.

"But you tried! You dressed up like me and you caused the distraction, yes? You sent a false urgent message?"

"Yes, but if you think upon it with Your Highness's obviously superior intellect, you will realize that I actually committed no crime."

"Yes, I'm much more highly intelligent than all the plebeians." She thought for several long moments. "Then you shall be given a trial. I am still not convinced you didn't steal them. But if 'tweren't you, then who?" She glared angrily at the crowd, which visibly cringed.

She stepped up to one of the guests who seemed particularly afraid and trembling with fear—a man wearing a mask. She pressed her nose to his. "Did you steal my tarts?"

"N—no, Your High-highness." He swallowed hard.

"I daresay you are much too nervous to not be guilty of *something!* Guards, off with his head! Take him away!"

Two guard cards dragged him, screaming, away.

The Queen of Hearts addressed the crowd. "Now, I shall ask each of you one by one, and have each of you executed until someone confesses!"

This caused a great deal of alarm, then everyone in the crowd began running away.

The Queen of Hearts watched and sighed. There were too many guests to be captured by her guards.

She looked down, lost in her misery. She had truly looked forward to eating those delectable tarts, but now that they were gone, it would take nearly an hour for the Cook to make her new ones.

She motioned toward the Knave. "Take him away to await his trial. And leave me alone." Her footsteps echoed through the large room as she walked to the table where her beautiful tarts had formerly been. The dome lay on the ground. The plate was empty. There were only a few crumbs.

She took off her mask and looked about to make sure she wasn't being watched. Sadly, she lifted the plate to her mouth.

And sadly she licked the crumbs.

THE KNIGHT

When Alice was 8

Alice was in her usual place when she wasn't running her rounds—in her hut, chained to her desk. At that particular moment, she was doodling on a piece of paper a picture of her punching the Cheshire Cat's floating head, when the door flung open with such a jolt against the wall that Alice shrieked and jumped. And even the guard card, who was usually such a sound sleeper, startled up from his nap. He did so with so much enthusiasm that the chair he sat in toppled over backward.

Alice looked in the doorway to see a knight in gleaming white armor holding a sword.

"White Knight?" she said, recognizing the armor from a previous encounter.

Meanwhile, the guard card was rolling on the floor and moaning. "Owey owey, I banged my head."

The knight pointed his sword and with his voice muffled behind the armor of his helmet, shouted, "Off with that!" or at least that's what Alice thought he might have said, muffled as his utterance was.

If the knight had indeed said "off with that!" she could only surmise that he meant the guard card's head. Perhaps that's how he hoped to cure the headache!

The guard card's eyes bugged out as he saw the sword pointed at him. "Uh oh!" He seemed to be looking around for his spear, which had rolled quite a distance away.

As the knight set his sword point down into the ground, Alice was hoping there wouldn't be a fight, because then she'd be forced to free herself from her chain and reveal her secret lock pick she'd made from one of her hairpins.

The knight took off his helmet. It was indeed the same White Knight Alice had encountered when she'd first come to this magical realm several months ago.

He was an older man with a white floppy mustache. He repeated himself, "I said, 'sorry about that'. I should have warned you before I made my dramatic entrance, good ol' chap."

"Who are you?" the guard card said as he was getting up.

"It's the White Knight!" Alice said, delighted.

The Knight looked at her. "I much prefer the term Light Knight now. It's much less limiting, don't you think?"

"If you say so, Light Knight. So what brings you here? Have you come to rescue me?"

The card had retrieved his weapon at this point. He pointed it at the Knight, but seemed hesitant to interrupt their conversation.

The Light Knight chuckled. "Ah, I would love to rescue you, my little damsel in distress. But rescue you from what?"

Alice lifted the chain in her hands, shrugged her shoulders and bugged her eyes. "Do you not see I am being kept captive? I am a damsel in distress, as you have said, being kept against my will here in Wonderland."

"Oh, balderdash," said the Knight. "What little girl wouldn't want to be in Wonderland? Why it is a magical world of fantasy and imagination!"

Alice scowled. She rattled her chains feebly.

The card meanwhile, shook his spear. "Pardon me. Excuse me. Hate to interrupt…"

The Knight looked at him. "Yes, my good man?"

"May I inquire as to whether you come here with good will or bad?"

"Ah, my apologies my good card! But I am here on the Queen's business. I have secured the young Alice's services for the accompaniment of me upon an important quest! She is to be my squire."

"Squire!?" said the card. He lowered his spear.

"That is correct. A most noble position indeed, in this most perilous, and heroic undertaking. Forsooth."

"What's a squire?" said Alice. "What is forsooth?"

"I'll tell you what a squire is. A squire is the knight's most valuable servant. The carrier of his weapons, the carer for his heart, who keeps his stomach full and his mind pure. Only the most specifically chosen can aspire to the greatness of the station. And..." The Knight took about a dozen clanking steps toward Alice. Unfortunately he tripped and fell, but managed to get up quickly enough. He lifted his sword in the air. "And...I choose you!" He brought the sword down with a vicious strike as Alice winced, but the sword struck on the chain links resting on the ground, severing them with a loud clank.

"Behold!" he proclaimed. "You have now been temporarily freed to be my servant!"

"Blimey," Alice muttered to herself as she lifted her arm that was still cuffed, with about four feet of dangling chains still connected.

The Knight pointed his sword at the dangling bits of chain, nearly gashing Alice's cheek in the process. "Oh that will not do." He whirled around ferociously upon his heel and barked at the card, "Do you have the key? My squire must be unlocked this instant!"

The guard card had suddenly grown meek. "Of course my liege." He set about putting his spear down so that he could pick up the keys.

Alice crinkled her eyes at him. "What makes you think I *want* to be your squire? Hmm?"

She held her wrist out as the card unlocked her.

"What? Praytell why *wouldn't* you want to? Honor! Heroism! Adventure! It's all there! Did I not mention we are going on a *quest?*"

Alice was rubbing her newly-unchained wrist. "A quest for *what*, then?"

The Knight sniffed. "A dragon. I wish to slay a dragon."

Both Alice and the guard card exclaimed simultaneously, "A dragon?!"

The Knight nodded solemnly. "A rival most vulgar and vicious. A dragon like no other. This dragon I daresay is a menace. The *ultimate* menace."

Alice pouted. "But I'm just a little girl. I fail to see why I should be called upon to battle menaces, ultimate or otherwise."

"Well, er." He fidgeted. "Maybe the dragon menace isn't *quite* as ultimate as all of that, then. The point of it is that you are exactly sufficiently capable of assisting me in my heroic aim."

Alice placed her fist upon her hip. "Again, I ask you, *why* exactly I would want to put myself in harm's way?"

"Well, because you're a good girl, correct?"

"Yes, I even have the two shoes to prove it." And here she showed him her shoes. He espied them with overmuch delight, she felt.

He said, "And dragons are ferocious and bad, and must be put a stop to, so of course you'd want to help, being the good little girl that you are."

Alice fidgeted and twerked her mouth from side to side, still not convinced.

"Besides, according to the script, you shall get to play the damsel in distress! Think of all the sympathy that will elicit!"

"Wait, what script?"

"Well, er, I mean to say, these quests tend to follow a particular sort of order. We wouldn't want to disrupt the natural progression?"

Alice huffed and stomped her foot. "So just because I'm a little girl, *I* have to be the damsel in distress?"

"Well," said the Knight, "you don't expect I should be her, do you?"

"Why can't you take someone else?"

"Because I need both a damsel and a squire, so who better than you? So have you decided to come?"

"I'm still thinking…" She tapped her chin. "What if *I* wanted to slay the dragon?"

"Ha, you couldn't harm a fly, even if you tried. We all know how meek and innocent you are. But enough of this piffle. We haven't the time for this. Why, right at this moment, the horrendous bloodthirsty dragon could be descending upon the village to pillage it and set fire to the fields and ravage the buildings with its vicious talons!" He was making clawy hands and had his eyes bugged out while making a scary face.

Alice drew back. "Oh my, that's awful!"

"Yes, so shall you accompany me so that I may successfully vanquish this threat in such a heroic manner that the bards shall sing of me? I've already composed a poem praising me. Would you like to hear it?"

"Oh no no," said Alice. "Save it for after you complete the vanquishing. That's when it'd be most appropriate."

He nodded. "Quite. Well, let's not dilly dally. Off we go on our quest. I'm afraid I can't allow any more time for you to decide. Are you coming?"

Alice rolled her eyes. "Well let's go then! Quit your dawdling!"

The guard card bowed at her. "I shall cancel your rounds for the day, milady."

"Thank you guard."

The Knight said, "My bag of weaponry and inventions is outside, but oh, one more thing, are there any extra chains about?"

"Why yes," said the guard card. "Why?"

The Knight answered, "They may come in quite handy when Alice plays the role of the Damsel."

Soon they were on their way. The Knight said they were traveling to a village that would be ravaged by the dragon, after which they would set out to the creature's lair to slay it.

"That's the natural order of such quests," he said.

Alice was huffing as she struggled to carry the clanking sack.

The flimsy sack ripped, spilling its contents onto the ground. She saw that the sack was merely a bedsheet. She looked woefully at the spilled supplies. She saw the extra pair of chains with lock and key, an odd cone-shaped device with a handle, a small pouch, a sword, a bottle of red liquid labeled "tomato catsup", a compass, a pair of goggles, what looked to be a cookie mold of a clawy creature's footprint, a box of matchsticks, bottle of rubbing alcohol, and a canteen."

"Here, I shall help you," said the Knight as he kneeled and his armor clanked. "Just retie the sheet, leaving out the part with the rip. It's the sword that seemed to have ripped it. Perhaps I should carry that."

"You think?! Why didn't you bring your horse? How far is this village anyway?"

"Well er, my horse and I recently had a spat. I'm sure he'll get over it. Of course I would have loved to have him with me for the trip to the faraway village, but seeing how I only have you, we shall go to a closer village."

Alice considered questioning him as to the logic of that, but thought better of it as she realized that a closer village would mean less walking and carrying for her.

They retied the sack and soon they were walking again. The Knight stopped answering Alice's questions or letting her in on any more information. He said that squires should be seen and not heard. At one point, the Knight realized that he'd left his helmet at the hut, but it was too late to go back. Alice giggled about that.

Soon they approached the "tea party" tree, beneath which was a table, where sat the three characters who sat there drinking tea all day. They were there as usual—the Mad Hatter, the Dormouse, and the March Hare.

"Ah," said the Knight. "There is the village that is to be attacked."

"Why that's no village. That's just the March Hare's tea table!"

"You should learn to complain less! I thought you wanted a village that was closer!"

"Yes. I apologize."

"Remember, seen and not heard."

The Knight clanked his way forward and Alice dragged the clanking sack/sheet of supplies upon the ground. She feared it would split again at any moment.

The Mad Hatter giggled and pointed. "Why it's the White Knight and Alice! Where's your horse, White Knight!?" The March Hare watched on quietly. Meanwhile the Dormouse had lain the side of his head upon the table, apparently taking a nap.

"Hello Mad Hatter, March Hare, Dormouse." He raised his sword dramatically into the air. "I have come—"

"Fancy a spot of tea?" interrupted the Mad Hatter.

"Perhaps in a bit," said the Knight. He wobbled the sword. "I hear his sepulchral wings beating upon the heavens. Hark, for here he comes!"

"Alice?" said the Mad Hatter. "Tea?"

"No thank you. I'm on a bit of a quest at the moment. Apologies."

"Quite all right," said the Hatter with a wave of his hand and a giggle. "Perhaps later."

The Knight shouted to be heard. "I have come to encounter the dragon that has been terrorizing this village, and then to track it back to its lair and slay it!"

The Hatter and March Hare looked around. Alice looked too.

"Dragon?" said the March Hare.

The Hatter said, "Village?"

"Yes!" said the Knight as he walked heroically up to the table with Alice following. "The horrible dragon that has been terrorizing this village. Do try to keep up shall you?"

Alice giggled at the puzzled expressions upon the Hare and Hatter's face. The Dormouse snored.

The Hatter said, "I say, my man, I thought I was the only mad one here."

The Knight proclaimed, "Oh, but I am the only one with the ears keen enough to hear the beating of the dragon's wings! Harken! He approaches! Soon he shall be here. Hand me my bag, won't you dear?" After she did so, he rummaged through it.

The March Hare began trembling. "Is a dragon truly coming to our village? To eat us?!"

The Hatter said, "As I said before, we are not a village. And a dragon has never attacked our village before. Why here? Why now?"

The Knight was adjusting the clear goggles upon his head now. He'd taken out the small pouch. "Ah, these goggles let me see into far distances." He shielded his eyes with his hand. "Ahah! There, off in the distance. I see it. Don't you?"

They all looked, except the Dormouse, who was still sleeping, but no longer snoring.

After they'd told him they saw nothing, the Knight sighed. "Very well, I see I shall have to point the vile bloodthirsty creature out. Soon he'll be close enough for all to see. Come, come everyone. Gather round. Come Alice, stand next to the Hare. There's a girl."

Alice didn't understand why they had to all huddle together in such a particular manner, but she went along with it. The Knight stood behind the three huddled voyeurs, then said, "Now look, just a little to the right of the sun."

They did so, but of course, the sun temporarily blinded them. The fierce brightness of it tinged all of Alice's vision with yellow. She heard the Hatter and Hare grunt and yelp as they too, apparently were similarly accosted by blinding light.

She heard a sifting sound behind her, like sand shifting through the air, then felt a pinging on her eyes, like irritating particles of dust. Then the bright blinding light in her vision suddenly shifted into pitch black darkness.

Behind them, the Knight shouted, "Oh no! The dragon has belched forth a blinding cloud!"

Alice heard the Hatter shriek and the March Hare called out, "I can't see!"

She rubbed at her eyes, but her vision remained pure black.

"Oh no!" called out the Knight. "The dragon is here! His claws, extended! He is about to rend you all limb from limb and roast you in his sulphurous dragon's breath of flame! And perhaps he shall eat you! He is fond of rabbit meat, I can tell!"

She heard the sounds of crashing china breaking upon the ground so she shrieked and instinctively covered her head with her arms and crouched, not knowing what else to do.

The March Hare called out, "Tell him I'm a hare, not a rabbit!"

While the Hatter yelled, "I can't see a thing! This is not desirable!"

To her left, she heard the Knight's voice call out, "Oh vile beast, leave this humble village alone, or suffer my wrath!"

Then a second voice from the left boomed forth in a deep voice, "Oh no, noble Knight, for I know you are the greatest knight of this land, and I shall burn you alive with my flaming dragon's breath, because you are so legendary and majestic, and then I shall burn this village to the ground!"

This caused issuances of lament from the Hatter and Hare. And Alice, in complete shock, could only utter, "No! Oh, no no no." The tears of her terror and helplessness began to well up within her blind eyes, then trembled over the edge of her eyes' boundaries and tumbled downward.

The Knight called out, "No, you shan't burn the little girl with your demonic breath's flame. She is my damsel in distress, so I shan't allow it!" And then she felt the tiny lick of flame upon her cheek. Alice shrieked and drew away from the heat. She could have run, but she was still blind, so how effective would such an action be?

The Knight called out, "I am swinging my sword at you, wretched dragon! Ow, you struck me in the eye! Now I attempt to strike you down, though I know I'll miss. Yes, that's right, retreat beneath my superior combat skills. Oh no! Now you are breathing your fire flame breath upon the table, immediately before you retreat back to your lair that I shall track you to. Oh no!"

Alice's sight suddenly returned—she realized it must have been the magic of her tears. She tried to get her bearings. The Knight had taken his goggles off and now had a black eye. She watched as he set a lit matchstick to the table, causing it to light on fire.

Alice's eyes bugged wide, but when the Knight possibly suspected and looked her way, she managed to shut her eyes once again and pretend to be still blind.

Alice still had her eyes closed. The Knight called out, "Ah, now the dastardly dragon has flown away, which signals the next stage of the quest. Everyone, I shall rinse your eyes out with water so that you may be able to see again. Ladies first." He guided her head back and she pretended to still be blind as he rinsed her eyes out with the canteen. She didn't want to embarrass the Knight by calling him out as a faker—she felt sorry for the old chap. *It must be hard being a knight with a lack of suitable adventures to be had.*

"I can see now!" Alice proclaimed. She looked at the Knight to see that now he had a bunch of blood upon his right cheek! Where had that come from if there was no dragon?! "You're hurt," she said.

"Pish posh. 'Tis but a scratch," he said courageously, and he went about reviving the sight of the others.

While he was rinsing out the Hare's eyes, the Dormouse rose up from the ground and yawned. Blandly, he said, "How did I get on the ground? Why is the table on fire?" He yawned.

Everyone ignored him.

The Hatter was furious. "My good knight, you must seek this dragon out and slay him so that he never visits our village again!"

"Hear hear!" said the Hare.

The Knight said, "Yes yes, that is exactly the next step I was about to undertake. My trusty squire and I must track the foul beast down!" He looked to the ground and knelt. "Look here! There are tracks here in the ground. I can use them to calibrate the dragon compass! Squire! Bring me the compass!"

Alice rummaged through the sack as all the others gathered around to look at the tracks. She noticed the cookie mold now had dirt clinging to it. On a whim she checked the catsup bottle to see that it had been opened. Alice pulled out the compass that looked like a normal compass that always pointed north. It even had the words of all the directions printed upon its face.

She handed the compass to the Knight then looked down at the tracks. They were identical to the cookie mold ones. She was no Sherlock Holmes, but she easily put two and two together.

The Knight put on a show for his audience. "Ah, now this compass is my own invention. All I have to do is calibrate it to the foul beast's tracks, and voila! It shall lead me and my squire right to the dragon's lair, where I shall heroically slay it. I've even written a poem to sing the praises of the event. Would you all like to hear it?"

They shook their heads. The Hatter said, "Perhaps later. After the actual slaying."

"Yes that would be the appropriate time," the March Hare said.

The Knight sniffed and looked disappointed. "Very well then. Squire! Follow me! Tallyho!" He began walking north, with Alice following.

"Is it far?" Alice whined as she lugged the heavy sack.

"Eh? Well no, it's not far. I know the perfect spot."

Inwardly, Alice was debating whether to call the Knight out. Because frankly he was lying and since she wore the goody two-shoes, Alice was very much opposed to lying. But she also didn't want to hurt the Knight's feelings. Perhaps it was one of those white lies she'd heard of. White lies from a white knight.

Soon they came upon a cave in the side of a hill.

"The compass points to that cave. That is where the ferocious dragon lives. I shall heroically enter the cave and impressively vanquish the beast despite our vastly different sizes. Then I shall recite my poem to you."

Alice rolled her eyes. "Shall I enter the cave as well, then?"

"Oh, no no. It is much too dangerous. You must stay outside, and listen as I wage battle with him." He was rummaging through the bag and brought out the bottle of catsup.

"Very well. You are so brave."

"I know." He raised his sword and called out to the cave. "Dragon! Prepare to be slain, for I, the Light Knight am here!"

He stumbled as he walked and dropped his catsup bottle, but then got up without comment and entered the cave. What ensued was the clanging of a most ferocious battle. Clanks and thuds issued forth. "Ow! You hit me hard that time! But now, look how I strike you! Oh, this battle has grown most feverish! How heroic I am to fight you! Ow! You struck me again! But look, I have struck you now. See how your blood drips upon my blade?"

"Oh for goodness sakes," Alice muttered to herself. "I have had quite enough of this foolishness."

Alice crept up to the entrance and peeked in, hiding as much as she could behind the edge.

She saw the Knight punching himself in the face inside a small cave that was filled with pots and pans. "Ow!" shouted the Knight. "You struck me a good blow that time. But you shan't be victorious!" He clanked his blood-covered sword onto a pot, making a loud clank noise. "There, take that blow!" He then punched himself in the face again. It was a solid blow, too, because he fell over unconscious onto the ground.

"Oh my!" Alice shouted. She rushed over to him. She would have hated for the Knight to have seriously harmed himself while fighting his imaginary dragon.

But she also knew she couldn't allow this charade to go on any further.

He didn't seem horribly harmed. After chaining his hands and feet together, she checked the blood on the sword. She tasted it. It was catsup. She roused him by softly slapping his face. "Wake up!"

"What? Where am I?"

"You managed to knock yourself out."

"Eh? You mean the dragon did."

"No, not at all. I know you were faking. It's bad to lie, you know! It's very unchivalrous."

"What? I did not! Where is the dragon? Did it flee?" He looked around.

Alice finally lost her temper and screamed in outrage and punched the Knight on the side of his face, but since she was only 8, it wasn't very forceful.

"Ow! I'm tender there!"

Alice immediately regretted her outburst. "Oh, I'm sorry dear!" She kissed his cheek. She looked at him. "It's just that it is not nice to lie. I can't allow you to keep up this charade."

The Knight looked back and sighed. "I know. It's just that...I wanted so bad to be a hero. I needed a monster to slay. I can't slay the Jabberwock, because we're friends, after all. There's just not enough monsters around here."

"What of the Bandersnatch?"

A frightened look came over his face. "You want me to be killed?!"

"No, I'm sorry. Of course not."

"Will you unchain me?"

"First you have to tell me how you tricked us. What inventions did you use?"

So he told her about the voice-distorting megaphone he'd used to disguise his voice and the blinding dust he'd blown into their eyes that would blind people for about ten minutes.

He tried to get up. "Now will you unchain me, please?"

"Not until you promise to confess to everyone."

"Confess?! That would be humiliating."

Alice nodded. She felt sorry for him. Then she had an idea. "Well, how about you give me that blinding dust and megaphone of yours so you can't use them on others, and we can both agree to never mention this thing with the dragon again."

"What? But I made a poem and everything!"

"Yes, I'm sorry, but you see, you didn't actually slay a dragon. You shouldn't brag about things you didn't do. Just say you couldn't find the dragon. It'll be a white lie."

"Oh very well then, you goody two-shoes! Can I at least tell you my poem?"

"That sounds pleasant." She unchained him—as she did so, she apparently wasn't paying enough attention, since she stumbled—why, her feet almost fell out from beneath her!

Then she had a change of heart as she fixed him with a look with her fist to her side. She was thinking about using the dust and megaphone for a little payback. "Now about the blinding powder…"

"Oh yes yes, you may have it. I have no further use for it."

"How long does the blindness last? It wouldn't be permanent would it?"

"No, it lasts ten minutes at the most. Now will you let me go?"

Alice agreed.

Before they left to go back to their respective abodes, the Knight recited the poem he had written about himself, which went thusly:

Oh, hear the tale of this brave knight,
Who smote the dragon in its lair.
The fearsome creature he did fight,
While others would have felt despair!

The dragon was so dangerous,
More fearsome than a bandersnatch,
And vicious and so devious,
But this day it had met its match!

To save the damsel in distress,
The knight faced claws and searing fire!
He is so brave, all must confess,
This lightning rod of girls' desire!

He smote it with a skillful strike,
He chopped it all to bits of gore,
This handsome knight who all girls like,
Then chopped it more and more.

So no, its head he hasn't brought,
But please to him, don't nag.
He's still the stud all girls have sought,
Although I hate to brag.

After the recitation, they went their separate ways. A few hours later, she discovered that the shoes she now wore weren't the goody two-shoes. The Knight must have switched them out unbeknownst to her. It seemed he was capable of some cleverness after all. But she hardly missed them, for she was very focused on paying a "special" visit to Humpty Dumpty.

HuMpty DuMpty

When Alice was 8

She snuck up on him carefully, from behind, in the cloak of night. At this time, Humpty Dumpty wouldn't be expecting her, and she was armed with just the right weapon. A non-fatal one: the blinding dust.

Payback time would soon come.

In one hand she held the voice-altering megaphone, with the other, she reached into a pocket of her ninja outfit for the pouch that contained the blinding dust. She wore goggles to protect herself from its effects. She'd also brought a small bag filled with the quick-rising cupcake mix she'd gotten from the Cook.

She was behind him now, kneeling just at the base of the low wall he liked to sit on top of. It really wasn't much of a wall, not very tall and not very wide—the

Queen of Hearts had taken his other, bigger wall away. He seemed to be talking to himself. He said, "Oh woe is me! Why did I do that to her, when I shall come to love her?! Oh, I hate having to be mean to her!"

Alice listened, with a puzzled expression beneath her mask. Who was he talking about? Surely, he couldn't be talking about she herself? But then again, he had earlier been mean to her by kicking her after she called him an egghead. He was sensitive about the fact he looked like a large egg with a face on it.

Now Humpty Dumpty moaned and whimpered and rocked back and forth. Alice had never seen this side of him—and she meant it literally, too, because he seemed on the verge of toppling over and landing on her, and then she would see the *in*side of him too! *But no, that's silly,* she thought. *Humpty is too experienced with sitting atop that wall of his to fall off so clumsily.*

With a woeful voice, he called out:

"I'm Humpty Dumpty, here on my wall!
I'm Humpty Dumpty and I cannot fall!
…into love, that is, for it will bring pain,
So I'll just stay heartless and full of disdain."

Alice was growing more and more confused. What was he going on about? Humpty Dumpty had never been the whiny lovesick sort. But here he was moaning privately about not wanting to fall in love? Well frankly, who would be the girl he fell in love with, and for that matter, who could possibly love that vicious jerk back?

"Oh I wish my dear Alice could just hurry up and kill me, so that I might love her again..."

This stopped Alice cold. He had just made an unintended confession to her. She almost wanted to call out to him, to ask him what he was going on about, but no, that would be humiliating for him, and she could never be that cruel to him. *Because I am Alice and through-and-through nice, although perhaps too nice.*

And that is why she could never bring herself to kill him, especially after seeing this sensitive, vulnerable side of Humpty.

Oh, she had started out *wanting* to kill him, to get her revenge, but she knew she would never be able to bring herself to go through with it.

She would have to settle for a cruel prank. That's why she'd liked the idea of the blinding dust. It wouldn't be permanent, so her conscience would hopefully be clear? Maybe? She felt such guilt for what she was about to do. And yet, she knew he deserved it.

And now he was whimpering while rocking and muttering. "Oh my Alice, someday, maybe someday. Someday..."

She was struck by a panic that he knew she was there. But as she listened, it seemed he was just talking to a hypothetical Alice. She was confused, but she decided she wouldn't waste anymore time trying to understand.

She waited for a good opportunity. Soon his mutterings dissolved and she saw that he was covering his eyes with his hands, completely lost in his misery.

Now was the time. She crept around the wall as Humpty said to himself, "But *why?* Why would I even want love when it brings so much pain?!"

She didn't stop to ponder the words.

She was up against the wall, right beneath him, so close, but he couldn't see her with his hands over his eyes. She lowered part of her mask, then brought a handful of the dust into the palm of her hand. She rose up with a handful of the powder and blew—whoof!—a cloud of dust into his face, then backed away a few feet.

She'd brought the megaphone in preparation for this moment and would have to remember to use it every time she spoke. As the cloud drifted over him, she uttered the words she had planned—her voice came out raw, guttural, and unrecognizable. "Someone you wronged sends their regards."

Humpty Dumpty yelped in surprise and drew back, but always the skilled wall-balancer, of course he didn't topple over. She had expected that.

He'd lowered his hands and the cloud had done its work. "I can't see!" he shouted out, obviously, because that was the whole point. He rubbed at his eyes, as she went about the second part of her plan.

As she brought out the small bag, she called up to him in her raspy megaphone voice, "And you never shall again." It was a lie, because the blinding dust would wear off within ten minutes.

"Who are you?" he called out, in anguish as he rubbed his eyes. "What do you want?"

As she sprinkled the chocolate-tinged quick-rising cupcake mix around the base of the wall, she couldn't help herself. Playing with her false voice augmented by the megaphone, she became ever-so-dramatic. "I am justice, here to right what you have wronged. I will break you!"

"What? How have I wronged you?!"

"Humpty Dumpty sat on a wall, Humpty Dumpty had a great fall." She said it in her scariest voice. In combination with the megaphone's effects, she sounded outright demonic.

"No, please!" he shouted. "Look, why don't we talk about this? I can give you something maybe? Maybe we can work something out."

Alice cackled. "There is nothing to work out. What goes up must come down. Cupcake arise!" The cupcake mix rose up instantly, forming a large cupcake surrounding the egghead's wall. The cupcake was topped with icing and was a couple of feet shorter than the wall, which stuck out from the middle.

"What is this under my feet?"

She ignored the question. "Why do you sit on that narrow lame wall anyway?"

Despite his obvious terror, he sneered. "None of your business!"

"Tell me or die!" she shouted in her voice that sounded outright demonic.

"Who are you? What do you want?"

"Are you afraid to fall?"

"What? Of course! Love is scary!"

"No, not fall in love." She huffed in frustration. Yet, her curiousity got the best of her. "What can you offer me to not push you off your wall?"

"Do you like Alice? I can give you a lock of blond hair I just this morning tore off her head."

And that's when Alice lost control, screaming like a banshee. "Awooo! I'll tell you, since you are as blind as a bat...I am about to push you off your lame pathetic wall! You won't survive, I fear. Oh well."

"What?"

"This is for Alice," she said.

She jumped and with both hands pushed him off the wall. He tumbled over while screaming in terror, and plopped into the sticky icing covering the plumpy cupcake.

She could hear him flailing and screaming for several seconds, but couldn't see him behind his wall.

"What?" he said. "Am I still alive?"

"Yes. You'll be okay if you just lie still. I just wanted to scare you. You're on a bed made of moist pastry."

"I can smell it," he said. "Chocolate."

"That's right. Be grateful I didn't kill you."

"And my blindness?" he said.

"Oh, that shall be permanent," she lied. "That's your punishment for being such a meanie head!"

"No!"

"Goodbye," she said, and with that she took off walking back to her hut.

"No! Come back! You mustn't leave me like this!"

She didn't respond.

"At least tell someone I'm stuck here!"

She stopped walking. She didn't feel as good inside as she thought she would. In fact, she felt quite yucky. She turned around and walked back to him. Unfortunately, she still had to use the megaphone, so her voice sounded soothingly demonic. "I'm sorry Humpty. You won't actually be blind forever. The powder will wear off in a few minutes."

Then she walked off, paying no heed to his calls asking who she was or his orders to inform others to help him.

She had stowed her usual black dress outside her hut and changed into it. She peeked into her hut to see that the guard card was still there in his chair snoozing away, and it was a simple matter to sneak back to her desk and fasten the chain back to her wrist using the lockpick she'd made from a hairpin.

It was just in time too, because just then the guard card woke up and stretched his arms.

Alice didn't wish to appear suspicious, so she rolled her eyes at him.

"Have a nice nap?" she said.

TWEEDLE TWINS

When Alice was 11

The Queen of Hearts was in the middle of a *perfectly* winning game of croquet, using that fool, obnoxious blowhard of a pink flamingo named Morley as her mallet, when in burst an interrupting guard card to break her concentration just as she was lining up her shot!

"My Queen! I have urgent news!" He prostrated himself face down upon the ground before her.

"Well now my shot is ruined!" she said, trying not to lose her temper. Nobody seemed to respect just how good a job she was doing of keeping it together, lately. She hadn't had anyone beheaded in three days.

"My apologies, Your Highness," the pathetic card whimpered into the ground.

"Well, now that you've interrupted my shot, tell me what the big emergency is then!"

"Yes, My Queen. It's just that the Tweedle twins—they're at each other's throats. They are going through a disagreement and are seeking a divorce of sorts, a divorce of brothers, you see."

"And so? What has that got to do with me?"

"It's just that they say you promised to be their judge if such a thing happened."

"Argh! So I did!" She set the pink flamingo Morley upon his feet. He all of a sudden, *now* chose to begin trembling. Shaking like a leaf, he was. "You're pathetic," she sneered to him, "just like your so-called 'poetry'."

Morley merely ducked his long neck and wobblingly exited the game field.

"Well, where are they then?" demanded the Queen.

The guard card said, "They await you in your throne room, along with the Cheshire Cat."

"Oh, that cat! Tell him I shall have him beheaded if he doesn't leave!"

She made her way to the throne room. There stood the chubby Tweedle twins, staring each other down while shaking their fist at each other.

"I'm so sick of you!" said one of the brothers. "Likewise!" shouted the other brother.

The Cheshire Cat's head was swirling around them in the air. The Cat had a habit of only materializing his head without his body, a tendency which severely irritated the Queen.

The twins were so engrossed in their argument that they failed to notice her entrance, which she found quite disrespectful. She considered having them executed on the spot.

Instead she shouted, "Your Highness is here, you nitwits!"

The Tweedle twins bowed. The Cheshire Cat sneered then went on displaying that creepily large grin of his. He was a most exceedingly rude feline. She would have to figure out a way to have him beheaded.

One of the twins said, "There's the Queen. Now you shall get yours." "Contrariwise! *You* shall get *yours!*"

The Cheshire Cat giggled. "Are you gonna let him talk to you like that?"

The Queen couldn't tell which twin he was speaking to.

She groaned. She desperately wanted to get back to her croquet. "You wish for Your Highness to preside over the proceedings?"

The Tweedle twins looked at her with a puzzled expression. The Queen felt that the boys just weren't all that smart.

The Cat said sarcastically, "Well that was some alliteration." The opposite of the twins, the Cat was *too* much of a smart ass.

The Queen groaned. "Why am I always surrounded by imbeciles? Tell me quick. What do you want me to decide? You want me as a judge?"

"Yes," said a Tweedle, "because I wish to get a divorce from *him.*" He pointed at his brother. "No, pay him no nevermind," said the other. "It is *I* who wish to be divorced from *him.*"

The Queen huffed. "A divorce? You're not married. But I think I know what you mean. But why now? You've always had your little tiffs before, but it's never come to this."

Tweedledee said, "The Cat informed me I shouldn't put up with this." Tweedledum said, "Nor *I* with *that.*"

The Queen sneered at the Cat.

In his bored-sounding voice, the Cat said, "Yes, I helped them see the hopelessness of their arrangement."

The Queen said, "Perhaps you shouldn't pay heed to the meddling of that horrid pussy cat. But okay, as I've got to get back to my game...your divorce is granted. Off with both your heads. Is that all?"

The twins' eyes went wide with alarm.

The Cat giggled and said, "Oh that sounds delightfully bloody!"

Tweedledum said, "No no, this is not a matter that involves execution." Quoth Tweedledee: "What he said."

"Oh fine then! You are both pardoned. Now I shall go back to my game." She began to walk away.

Behind her, one of the twins said, "Wait. We want you to divide our property." "Yes," said the other, "give part to one, part to the other."

The Queen was by this time fuming. She had a short temper, and these two bumbling fools were trying her patience, not to mention that obnoxious cat rubbing his non-executed status in her face with his floating head.

"What property? You have no property."

They pointed to the ground where rested their child's rattle. It was the very same rattle the Queen had given them a year earlier for bringing the Red Queen in.

She said, "Fine then! What is the grounds of your divorce? Your Highness must determine who is at greater fault."

Tweedledee explained, "We had an agreement that *I* should lick the tears from Alice's right eye and he from the left."

"'Tweren't neither! Her left is oftimes not *my* left!"

"Are you to tell me," she said, her cheeks turning red, "that this is all over you two not being able to tell which way is left and which way right?"

The Cat was chuckling.

Tweedledee said, "Sometimes *my* right is not *your* right." Tweedledum said, "And sometimes her left is not *my* left."

The Cat said, "So who gets the rattle?" with an obnoxious arch of his brow.

The Queen said to him, "I don't like how smug you are. I hereby sentence you to death. Off with your head!"

"Good luck since I have no body, therefore I can't be beheaded."

"Argh! I am quite tired of all of you! Now I have the solution. Here is my judgment…"

The twins leaned forward, listening.

The Queen said, "The rattle shall be divided in half. You each shall get a piece. There, your divorce settlement is resolved."

The boys burst into tears. "But we love our rattle!" "I love it more than him!"

The Cat helped, "Why not divide the *twins* in half instead."

"That's something worth considering," the Queen said to him.

"I take it back!" wailed Tweedledum. "Likewise," said Tweedledee. "I wish to have the divorce annulled!" "As do I!" "I want to more than him!" "No, I do!" They glared at each other. Their hands formed into fists.

The Queen rolled her eyes. "Very well then! The divorce is annulled. Your precious rattle shall remain intact. Now that you have wasted my time, I order you not to do so again. From now on, you shall settle your disputes amongst yourselves, or I shall have you executed. Understand?"

"Yes, quite." "I daresay I understand more than him."

The Queen nodded slowly, then burst into a fit of action—while screaming, she rushed toward the floating Cat's head and tried to punch him with all her might.

But he swooped out of the way. "You'll have to be faster than that," he said with a chuckle.

The Queen, furious, shouted, "Oh get out of my sight, the obnoxious lot of you!" She turned and walked back to the croquet grounds, hoping that the flamingo named Morley hadn't slinked too far away.

The Witch Doctor

When Alice was 9

When Alice was 9-years-old, she went through a particularly dark and mournful period. She was woeful of the horrible treatment from all the creatures of Wonderland and resentful that she was being held captive there. She grew so woeful that she slept most of the day and went about her rounds slowly and unsmiling. She hardly seemed to react to things at all, and for that reason, the citizens of Wonderland began to find her a bore.

It was harder to make her cry, to shriek and show fear. Utterly boring, she was. And inside, she was consumed with dark thoughts, of sadness, hate, loneliness, and particularly troubling, a desire for revenge. But all those dark emotions were so overwhelming that she just ended up, ironically, feeling numb and hopeless.

At that particular moment, she was standing beside the Queen of Hearts in her game room, beside one of her newest toys, a billiards table. Since Alice was 9 and short, she had to stand upon a crate to be able to reach. She woefully held a pool cue in her hand, staring at her feet.

Next to her, the Queen of Hearts said, "You're not paying attention to me, my girl!"

Alice woefully raised her head, with its precious blond locks. "Sorry," she muttered. The Queen had already taught her much of the game, with the understanding that once she learned how to play, Alice would be expected to either lose every time or lose her head. Since she was only 9, she thought it would be easy to lose.

This day, they had an unusual guest—a man known as the Witch Doctor, who had come from a foreign land in a foreign continent or island or somesuch. He was completely bald and had a bone going through the middle of the inside of his nose, which Alice found quite curious.

The Queen said, "Now, what do we call this again?" She pointed at the white ball.

"A cute ball," Alice said, then sighed.

"No, no! It's called a cue ball! Now watch carefully. I have already showed you how to jump the ball."

"Light a fire under its bum," Alice said. That's how the Queen had described it—according to her, she liked to imagine the cue ball was an enemy whom she was sneaking behind and lighting a fire to. The Queen seemed to have many violent thoughts associated with what was merely a game. When she referred to the act of knocking the other balls into the pockets, she likened it to "pushing enemies into their graves".

"That's right," said the Queen. "Now for your next lesson, I'd like to teach you how to apply english to the cue ball."

"If she can manage to do it properly…" muttered the Witch Doctor quietly, just loud enough to be heard.

The Queen turned to him. "What was that?"

"Nothing, Queeny, I was just saying you can do it most properly."

She glared at him for a few moments as if deciding whether to believe him, then finally said, "Quite."

The whole exchange caused Alice to give forth a slight giggle, a rare occurrence these past few melancholy weeks.

The Queen looked back to Alice with an expression on her face that seemed to indicate she was sick of looking at the Witch Doctor.

Alice said, "Apply English to it? Do you mean to give a stern talking to it?"

The Queen tutted condescendingly. "No, my silly girl. Although, I can understand your confusion. No, it is an entirely different use of the word than you're

thinking of. Some people refer to it as 'applying spin'."
She leaned and edged the tip of her pool stick toward
the cue ball and prepared to make her shot. "What it
refers to is hitting the cue ball at an angle so that, as it
moves forward, it spins. You tap it hard with the stick—
boom!—and give it a twist. I like to think of it this way:
it's much like the cue ball is the head of someone you
despise, and bam!!! You snap their neck with a twist and
send their head rolling to knock the other persons, I
mean balls, into their graves, I mean pockets."

Alice had jumped when the Queen had loudly
shouted, "Bam!!!"

"Yikes," the Witch Doctor muttered, again just barely
decipherable.

"What was that?" the Queen snapped as she again
jerked her head to him.

"I meant yikes, you are astounding in the degree that
you have mastered this game."

Alice once again tittered despite herself. She thought
the Witch Doctor was a bit too feisty and sarcastic for
his own good. Didn't he realize that the Queen regularly
beheaded people and creatures for much less?

The Queen waggled her finger at him. "Watch
yourself. You've got a mouth on you."

"I shall," he said, but it looked more like he shan't.

The Queen huffed and turned back toward Alice.
"Now after enough practice, when you apply your
english to the ball, you can do all sorts of wondrous
things. For example, you can cause the cue ball to curve

in its path. Or, by using the proper amount of spin, you can cause the other heads, I mean balls, to twist in a certain way once they are struck. It's most marvelously complicated, don't you think, my girl?"

"Yes, Your Highness," Alice answered automatically, but the words felt empty. Her whole life had seemed to be a vacuous exercise in futility, she thought morosely.

The Queen continued, "I like to imagine that these balls are all heads that I have myself all ordered to be decapitated. Now watch." She applied some chalk to the tip, then with her pool cue, she struck the cue ball at an angle so that it curved, going around a striped ball and curving around to strike a green solid-colored ball which then sailed into a corner pocket.

"Aha!" shouted the Queen victoriously. "When heads shall roll, the Queen of Hearts is always in control!"

"Congratulations," Alice said glumly. Her thoughts briefly reflected on the cue ball—if the Queen considered it a head upon a neck being snapped, how could it then also be a bum beneath which a flame was lit? That seemed biologically impossible, but she failed to mention the discrepancy, because her melancholy discouraged it.

The Queen seemed to notice her lack of talkativeness. "Is that all you have to say? No clever quips?"

"No, My Queen," she said then clamped her mouth.

"Why my girl, I say, you're no fun at all anymore. So I have appointed this Witch Doctor here to fix you."

She waited for Alice to give the appropriate response of saying, "Fix me?" but Alice merely remained woefully silent.

The Queen said, "The Witch Doctor here is quite clever himself, though he lets his mouth get away from him at times. He shall be your mental aid, like a psychiatrist. Ha! A veritable head shrinker!" She began to laugh out loud and the Witch Doctor began tittering along with her.

Puzzled, Alice queried, "Your Majesty?"

The Queen said, "Well I made a bit of a joke there. You see, the magic wielders of his tribe have acquired the ability to shrink decapitated heads down to quite small sizes. It is really quite amazing. I have been asking him to teach me how to do it."

"I doubt you could do it right," he muttered, again under his breath.

"What was that?!"

"I mean, at *first,* Your Majesty. It is a most difficult procedure, but I'm sure, given enough time, even *you* could learn how to do it properly."

She scowled at him for a moment. "You should watch yourself—you're not as cute as this girl here. She is allowed to say things that *you* are not. But lately she has been as silent as a mouse, and so she is failing to entertain Your Highness sufficiently. So, Alice, I'm sending him home with you, my girl, to fix you with his primitive magic." She turned to him and growled. "And you best fix her or it's off with your head."

"I highly doubt that," he muttered.

"What was that?"

"Nothing, Your Highness."

"Oh, be off with you two. I've had enough of you for one day, Witch Doctor. You irritate me."

And so Alice and the Witch Doctor returned to Alice's hut. Alice dutifully chained herself to her desk, since the guard card who usually did it was away.

It started out rather awkwardly. Alice sat at her desk staring at this strange bald man.

"How did you do that?" she asked as she pointed at the bone through his nose.

He told her the painful process, which included pressing a sterilized needle through the tissue inside the nose, and Alice pulled faces and winced.

But afterword, she said, "It looks quite fetching though, in a primitive manner."

"Why thank you, young miss. I've heard of you. Young Alice the girl from the outside world with the magical tears. I have quite a propensity for magic myself. I make potions and perform spells."

And here he filled Alice in on all he could do. He told her how he could cast curses, could perform spells for good luck, bad luck and love, he even knew the formula for a potion that would convert a person into a will-less slave known as a zombie.

At the look of Alice's horror, he reassured, "But don't worry, I wouldn't zombiefy such a pretty young girl such as yourself."

At this she nodded and sighed, lost once more to her melancholy.

He observed her. "Ah yes, a dark cloud has passed over your spirit, stealing you of your mojo, yes?"

She sighed. "I don't know what mojo is, but I think I might be lacking it, yes, kind sir Witch Doctor."

"Ah, well I have been summoned here to help you, sweet child, but to do so, I must know more. Can you tell me what is wrong?"

"I'll tell you what it is. I am a bad girl."

He arched a brow. "How so?"

"I have dark thoughts, I am ashamed to say. I used to be able to push them aside, but lately they've been overwhelming. Why, these thoughts are horrifying..."

"Are you going to cry?"

"What? No, I don't think so."

"So tell me about these thoughts."

"Well, the other creatures of Wonderland are so cruel to me, and though I try to stay a nice good girl and still keep love in my heart for them, sometimes, I just...have these visions in my head, of getting revenge, even though I know it is wrong to seek it."

"I see. What kind of visions?"

"Oh Witch Doctor, they're horrible! Why, I want to punch them and kick them and beat them and flay them and cut them and choke them!"

"Choke them?"

With wide eyes she said, "Oh yes, and cut them and disembowel them and strangle them and—"

"Well you already said cut them."

"And bust their kneecaps and snap their necks and pull their hearts out of their chests and show it to them before they die."

"Before or after you snap their necks?"

"I would perform those acts separately to two different individuals."

"Oh I see. Those are indeed dark thoughts."

She looked at him with eyes wide with sincerity. "Oh yes, Witch Doctor, they most certainly are! The thoughts have brought this black cloud over me, as you call it, and everyday the darkness rains upon me and enshrouds me in the sickly trickles of melancholy."

"Oh my, dear child, that is quite poetic."

"Thank you. I actually did even comprise a poem about it:

Oh, dark cloud of melancholy,
I feel you descend, and now embracing me.
I breath in deep your tempting wisps,
And feel you tingle upon my lips.

I mingle with your tendriled tongue,
Forgetting that I'm still too young,
For dark desires, of vengeance brought
To those who only their own pleasure, sought.

I yearn to fill their souls with fears,
To feast upon their trembling tears,
To serve at hatred's beck and call,
To bring their broken neck and fall.

"That was the poem revealed to me in a dream. What do you think it all means?"

"I think it means you are a very disturbed little girl. But I know how to help."

She almost smiled. "Oh? That would be delightful."

"Yes, I anticipated your problem, so I made sure to bring this." He reached into a leather satchel at his side. He brought out a cloth rag doll in a black dress, with X's instead of eyes, and her mouth hand-stitched. The doll was lacking hair, though. It had a corruptagram pendant around its neck. The corruptagram is a symbol of a broken heart inside a circle with devil horns on top.

Alice said, "Ooh, I must say that's a rather ugly doll."

"It's a hate doll."

"Oh my, it reminds me of a thing I read of in the penny dreadfuls referred to as a voodoo doll."

"Well my girl, they are similar but not quite the same. They both make use of pins, though." He brought out a pin cushion shaped like a miniature head.

Alice gasped.

"Oh don't worry, this shrunken head is fake."

"Is it true that you know how to shrink a head down to such a small size?"

"Oh yes, but it requires preparation—first you must remove all the bones inside, then you have to apply heat to the head until it shrinks."

She wrinkled her nose. "That seems outright ghastly, but I should like to try it upon some of these vile Wonderland creatures." She scowled, then raised her fist and shook it. Then she sighed. "Those dark thoughts again. This hate doll can help me?"

"Yes, listen up. What you can do is take all of those hateful thoughts of revenge and maiming and transfer them to your hate doll by sticking the pins in it. You will then move your hatred from within yourself and pin it to your doll. The doll will wear your hate for you, so you won't have to carry it inside, you see? Then you will go on being that sweet girl you were before. Show me that smile."

Alice made an effort to smile.

"Ah there we are. All those bad feelings will no longer plague you and your dark cloud will blow away, poof! But there is one condition."

"Yes?"

"Well in order for the magic to work, I shall need to strip you of your hair and fasten it to the doll's head, in order for it to be your magic representative."

She clasped her long blond hair reflexively. "My beautiful hair? Is that truly necessary? I do so love my hair!" She felt on the verge of tears.

"Oh, there we are," he said as he glanced at those brimming potential droplets.

He began rummaging through his satchel again.

She grew indignant and sniffled. "You're supposed to tell me, 'don't cry' then try to console me!"

He brought out a little hollow glass tube with a cork sealing it. "Oh, my apologies. I don't know how to console you though. There is no other way. But you'll feel much better after you get rid of your hate. And your hair will grow back, of course."

Alice sighed. She now felt too emotionally numb even to cry. "Fine. Whatever."

"Very well. I have a kind of lotion that I will rub on your scalp. After a few moments, all your hair will fall out and you shall be as bald as, well, me, or a cue ball."

Alice merely nodded meekly, and peered forlornly at the top of her desk as he rummaged. Soon, he had brought up a little container, which he unscrewed then began slathering the noxious goo into her scalp like shampoo, while she sat with her hands resting in her lap, no emotion upon her face.

It began to tingle and feel warm amongst her follicles. The Witch Doctor snarled and grabbed a hold of her hair and twisted, but it hadn't yet detached from her head and she yowled. "Ouch! That hurts!"

"Oops, sorry." He looked into her eyes, which had wettened from the sudden pain. "Go ahead, cry. I shall collect your tears."

Then with a fizz and snap, her hair broke free. He chuckled. Alice shrieked. "You bastard! I'll kill you!"

He was standing in front of her, smugly holding her golden locks. "If you say so, baldy."

Alice scowled, then she shook her head. "No, it is wrong to want to harm others. That is why you must help me!"

"If I do, will you *please* muster up a few tears, my girl? For my potions. If you do, I'll even cast a temporary skill-increasing spell that will allow you to beat the Queen in billiards. Okay?"

"Ha! I would love to see her face when I beat her. No, I mean, it would make her oh-so-sad to lose. That would be mean, and it'd be like cheating."

He arched his brow while staring at her.

Self-consciously, Alice raised her hand and ran it over the top of her head—yes, it was bald and smooth, it almost felt like it was waxed. She pulled a face.

"Well, okay, my girl, if you do not wish me to cast the spell, then I shan't…"

Alice nodded. But then she felt them coming on again—the dark thoughts. She tried to fight them off, but they were too strong. "No! Do it, before I change my mind! Ha! I want her to suffer humiliating defeat! I promise I'll cry for you!"

"As you wish, milady." He rummaged, brought out another liquid-filled tube. He grinned. "I managed to obtain some of the Queen of Heart's sweat while she was playing billiards with me." He opened it with his mouth, since he still held her hair in his other hand. "I shall now sprinkle her sweat upon your cue ball head…there we are. And now I shall place my hand upon your smooth head. Now don't squirm, my dear. And now I shall recite some words in my native tongue." He launched into a guttural chant in a language unfamiliar to Alice. "And voila!" He removed his hand. "Now, whenever you play billiards during the next few days, you shall be highly skilled and able to make the most astounding shots! It will be near impossible for you to lose! And now that that's done, let us move on to the matter of you unburdening your dark thoughts, shall we?"

Alice nodded. "Quite right."

After some more rummaging, the Witch Doctor produced a band to tie Alice's former hair with, then he brought out a jar of glue he used to stick the hair onto the doll. As they waited for the glue to dry, the Witch Doctor handed the bone pins to her. "Now listen up, my girl. What you shall do is, you shall place one hand to your heart and hold a pin with the other. Then you shall bring up all those dark hateful thoughts of revenge and cruelty. With my aid, those dark thoughts shall transfer to the pin, which you shall then stick to the doll version of you."

"Where shall I stick it?"

"Why, to the doll's heart of course. There, you see?" He pointed to the doll's chest, where there was a red heart painted. "You shall empty your heart of your hatred and transfer it to the doll's heart, where it shall be kept. Then you shall be free from those thoughts!"

"Oh my! Such strange magic indeed! What would happen if the pins were removed from the doll?"

"Well, then those dark thoughts would be freed, so I suggest you don't let that happen. Even so, the effect won't last forever, for you are capable of growing new hateful thoughts to replace the old ones."

"Oh no no. I learned my lesson. I shall once again strive hard to remain a good little girl, who bears no ill thoughts toward anyone! I won't even let such notions begin!"

"Er, if you say so. All I care about is getting ahold of some of those precious tears of yours. We have a deal, right?"

"Oh, yes yes." She waved her hand. "Let's get on with it, then."

And so Alice did as instructed. As she was about to stick the first pin in, the Witch Doctor encouraged her: "Now focus on your thoughts of revenge. What would you like to do to the Queen of Hearts, and the Tweedle Twins, and all the other rascals who torment you every day? Hmm?"

Alice closed her eyes and brought the hatred up from her heart. "I would love to stab them and cut them, then maim then barbecue them then behead them then feed them their own barbecued heads!"

"That's it! Gorge on your hate! I love it." He made some chants and hand movements, then Alice felt some of the hateful feelings shoot from her heart up her chest, then down her arm and into the pin. "Now stick the needle in!"

Alice stuck it into the doll heart, then felt some of her hatred lessen. She repeated the procedure four more times, and each time the dark thoughts lessened until they were gone completely and each time the heart on the doll darkened until it was black.

Alice took a contented sigh and grinned big. "Ah, now I feel most lovely. I am my old self again. I harbor no ill thoughts towards anyone anymore!"

He peered at her. "Well, that's great. But there is still the matter of my tears you promised me." He stared at her eyes, but there were no tears brimming there.

"Oh yes," Alice said. "I remember, but I'm just so dang gummed happy, I have no tears right now." She hugged herself and squeezed while squealing with delight. Then she pounced on the Witch Doctor and hugged him. "Oh, you're my hero!" she shouted.

He pushed her off. "Oh that's enough of that, my girl! Now I must make you cry. You promised me!"

He glared at her. She shrunk back and said, "You like making little girls cry?"

He grinned menacingly. "I, my dear, love it." He slapped her hard across the face.

She screeched at that and pressed her hand to her face. "Ow! That hurt!"

"It was meant to," he sneered.

"That wasn't nice!"

"I know. But I don't fear you at all. I know you won't do anything about it. All your dark thoughts were stored away in that doll. Don't you miss them?"

"No," she said, with her eyes brimming with tears, but she didn't cry, "for I know I am pure of heart. I don't know what is going on with you. We all make mistakes, after all. I forgive you."

The Witch Doctor just stared at her for a moment, then rolled his eyes. "My, what a virtuous girl you are. But I don't have time for this nonsense. I must get back to the Queen to inform her that I have fixed you." He took a moment to take in her bald head. "Why, you used to be such a pretty little girl." He made a tsk sound with his mouth. "But now, I daresay, your appearance is…below par." He began rummaging in his bag again. Pulled out a hand-held looking glass, then held it up so she could see her reflection.

Alice stared in horror at the bald-headed version of herself.

Softly, he said, "Think of it. All your beautiful golden hair is gone. Think how long it will take to grow it back. The situation is utterly dismal, I'm afraid."

Alice's lower lip began to tremble.

The Witch Doctor said, "The leaves have fallen from the tree. The chicken has been plucked of its feathers. I hate to say the word, 'ugly', so I shall refrain from doing so. Your hair, your beautiful hair, is gone."

And that, as they say, is the straw that broke the camel's back. The levee broke and the tears were unleashed.

And in an instant, he was there to encapsulate and enslave a few of those sacrificial tears to the glass cages of his cork-topped tube.

Once he had scooped up the tears he wanted, and given her the bone she asked for, he made a quick exit. Leaving Alice all alone, but at least her heart was no longer burdened by dark thoughts, and she began to hum and sing, just an angelic sweet little girl once again.

The next day, she went to visit the Queen of Hearts at her billiards table once again. The Witch Doctor was absent this day.

As Alice approached, the Queen of Hearts pulled a face, and said, "Yick! What happened to you?!" for Alice looked quite different from yesterday.

Her head was still bald, but also, during the night, she'd grown curious and had used the Witch Doctor's lessons to stick a bone through the inside middle of her nose.

"Good morning, Your Highness!" She beamed.

"Why you look like that Witch Doctor, except much shorter."

"Yes, I've never had a bone in my nose before. Speaking of the Witch Doctor, where is he?"

"Oh, he shall be along shortly. Yesterday he annoyed me quite too much, and I got so angry that I couldn't tolerate him anymore, but I cut him down to size. He shall no longer speak to me in such a rude manner. But he told me that he had fixed you?"

"Oh yes!" she said with a giggle. "I took all those bad thoughts and stored them away!"

"Ah yes, on the doll, correct?"

"Yes. It is a most ugly, yet glorious doll."

"I shall be wanting that doll. Where is it?"

She pouted. "It's at my hut. But what use do you have for a doll? You're a grown up."

She folded her arms. "Because I want it, and I get what I want."

Alice pouted again, but then she tried to think of why the Queen would want it. Maybe the Queen was sad because she had no toys! "Well, I hope it makes you happy, Your Highness!"

The Queen chuckled. "I daresay you *have* been cured, my child."

"Thanks!"

The Queen rolled her eyes. "But I'm afraid that non-hairdo of yours *shan't* do. I shall have someone whip up a special potion that will speed-grow your hair, but it shall come in black..."

"Ooh, pretty."

"Quite. Now, let us play a game shall we? There is your crate. But first, I don't think I can *bear* to look at your bare noggin' a second longer! Why I can see my reflection in it!"

"You can?" Alice pressed her hand self-consciously to her head.

"Not literally. I was just mocking you."

"Ohhh."

"Now, I have come up with a solution for your ugliness until your hair grows out again. Guard!" One of the guard cards stepped forward, holding a wig of long black silky hair, which he handed to the Queen. "Ah, here we are. Now stand up on your crate so I can put it on you."

After a few moments, the wig was adjusted upon Alice's head.

The Queen handed her a pool cue. "Now let us begin the game, shall we? I shall break."

Alice tried to remember the rules. What the Queen was doing was called racking the balls. All the balls started out in a triangle. She removed the rack. Next, the Queen would hit them with the cue ball, which Alice didn't see on the table.

Reading her mind, the Queen said, "Ah, I have it right here. We shall play a slightly different game today." She was reaching down at the side of the table. "I told you the Witch Doctor would be joining us, and here he is…" She brought up an object in her hand and set it on the table.

Alice squinted down, trying to make sense of it. It looked a most curious ball. It was not completely smooth and round.

She gasped. "Crikey! It's the Witch Doctor's head!" She stared in horror at it—the eyes were sewn shut, and it looked slightly more wrinkly than it had been when it had been normal-sized, but there was the bone in his nose, just like the one she wore.

The Queen sniffed. "It seems to be, yes. I'm glad he taught me the whole head-shrinking business. It *was* a bit tricky, but I managed well enough."

"Why did you do that?"

"Because he mouthed off to me." She hit the shrunken head with her pool cue, and it rolled wobbily and hit the side of the triangle of balls with a thud. It obviously hadn't struck where the Queen had intended.

"Oh bollocks," the Queen of Hearts said as the balls lazily separated. "I'm afraid his head doesn't make a very good ball. I had to put lead on the inside to give him some heft." None of the balls had gone into a pocket. "But do the best you can my dear."

"Oh I shan't! He was my friend! He helped me!"

"He was a rude obnoxious jerk! Now you shall play, or you shall rue your disobedience. Now it is your turn! You must hit the cue ball."

Alice struggled to hold back her tears and calm her frantic breathing. "Yes, My Queen." She repositioned her crate then stood upon it again.

"Do you remember my lessons?" said the Queen.

Alice nodded meekly. Her lower lip trembled. She was thinking about the poor poor Witch Doctor.

"Go ahead, then, make your shot."

Alice looked down at the head, then looked away. She couldn't bear it.

The Queen encouraged while she pointed. "See that ball? You have a straight shot. Remember the poem?"

Alice nodded. Quietly she muttered:

"Strike it straight on when you're making your shot,
To make it roll in a path that's direct,
Or strike at an angle at just the right spot,
To make it twist just like you're snapping a neck!"

"That's right. Go on then..."

Alice closed her eyes and wildly poked the cue sticky thingy out. It struck the cue head and then she heard a ball roll into a pocket.

She opened her eyes. She'd hit the ball in!

"Wow, you did it! With your eyes closed and everything! It must be beginner's luck."

"Can I stop now, Your Highness? I don't like striking my former-friend's head. It seems somehow disrespectful."

"No, we can't let your lucky shot be the last of it, can we? I want to see you miss one. Why you're just an amateur. And here we'll see it proven." She pointed to the balls. "Now look where your cue ball head is positioned. Since you are now stripes, you must hit another stripe in, but look, the cue ball is against the edge there, see, and its way is blocked by all those solid balls. If you are to hit the stripe in, you must make the cue ball curve. Do you remember how?"

"Yes'm."

"Very well. Now move your crate. There is no way you shall make this shot. You haven't got the skill. But we must fail in order to eventually succeed, yeah?"

Alice set the crate down and stood on it. "Yes, My Queen." She positioned the pool stick.

"Remember from the rhyme?"

"Yes. Strike at an angle at just the right spot, to make it twist just like you're snapping a neck!" She closed her eyes and struck out wildly with her pool stick.

The stick connected with the miniature head—she heard a bunch of balls clacking and bouncing and dropping into baskets.

The Queen exclaimed, "Impossible!"

Alice opened her eyes to see that she had sunk every single striped ball into a pocket. The shrunken head was in the middle of the table upside down and facing away from Alice.

Alice giggled. "Wow, that was easy."

The Queen scowled and tromped over to Alice. "Give me that," she said as she yanked the pool cue from Alice's hand.

Alice yelped, "What?" in surprise.

"Your Highness does not wish to play this game anymore. Now begone with you. I'm tired of looking at your boney face!" In a huff, she grabbed up the shrunken head and stormed out of the room.

Alice sighed. She hoped she hadn't hurt the Queen's feelings by playing so well. She shrugged, then prepared to go about the rest of her rounds. She had a certain amount of creatures and people she had to visit each day. She hoped she could put a smile upon their faces, now that her dark thoughts had been stowed away.

MaD HaTTER

When Alice was 11

Alice was going about her daily rounds of ridicule and humiliation. She had just come from her session with the Tweedle twins. She had to keep telling herself the twins didn't know any better. It was a good thing that a couple years ago she'd stored all her hateful thoughts away in a voodoo doll, but slowly she'd been growing more dark thoughts, so she often had to remind herself to be nice to others.

Next up on her agenda was a visit with the Mad Hatter. He wasn't as cruel as many of the other citizens of Wonderland. Most of the time he merely liked to stare at her creepily. He'd requested that today she meet him at his hat workshop.

Alice had a bit of a soft spot for him. He was actually quite handsome and dashing in his exquisite hats, but he was also quite mad, from all the chemicals he used to make his hats, it was rumored.

She watched as the door of his workshop opened and the Mad Hatter came out, not wearing a hat on his head, but holding one in his hands, though. He looked more off his rocker than usual, in fact he looked outright raving mad. His eyes rolled about and his head lolled from side to side.

"Aaaliiicccee," he said. "I've been awaiting anxiously." He staggered toward her—he nearly stumbled.

"I say, Hatter, are you alright? You seem out of sorts."

He was standing in front of her now, blinking rapidly while twitching. She could see now that his face glistened with a heavy sweat. "My apologies for being quite more mad than usual, milady, but I've been working on a very special hat. It required such precise calculations, exotic techniques, and such concoctions and chemicals, why…they seem to have really affected me!" He waved his free hand and twitched.

She looked down into the top hat—she was staring at the inside of it, lined with soft felt. "Is that the hat?"

"Yes!" he shouted louder than necessary. "If I don't die, you shall wear it."

She thought he might be joking, but when she looked in his eyes, he seemed serious. "Oh no, Hatter. Really?"

He nodded gravely and twitched.

Tears welled up in Alice's eyes. "Oh, I don't want you to die!"

"I want you to cry into it!" he screamed, sounding terrified.

"What?"

"Now!" Roughly he grabbed the back of her head and slammed her face into the hat. Granted it was soft, but still she gasped. Some of her tears were flicked into it. "There, there," he said. "Yes, it shall all work now. I mustn't panic." Then he looked at her and his eyes went wide. "Ahhhh!!"

"What?!" She felt her face with her fingertips. "What is it?!"

He drew back and began looking madly about. "No! It's all in my mind!" He sobbed and whimpered. He was so out of sorts that he dropped the hat.

Alice rushed over to him. "Calm down. It'll be alright."

The Hatter's face was contorted in fear and he was shuddering all over. "Help me," he whimpered. His legs gave out and he fell and sat upon the ground.

Alice felt so horribly sorry for him. She placed a steadying hand upon his shoulder as she kneeled. "It's just the chemicals affecting your mind. Don't worry. You're safe."

"It's terrible! I don't think I can stand it! Please... please...help me." He looked at her with pitiful pleading eyes.

"How can I help?"

"Please," he said, sounding like a small child. "Please just hold me…"

So she wrapped her arms around him and held him close. "There there," she said softly. She cradled his head. "Shh, it'll be okay, sweetie."

He wrapped his arms around her and whimpered as the shudders shook through his frail body.

And she held him tighter.

She rocked him from side to side as his shudders and sobs lessened.

The Hatter was quiet now, breathing evenly as she held him.

Alice said, "I love you, Hatter."

He grunted.

"Do you love me?" she asked, feeling vulnerable.

"I think you're very pretty."

"But do you love me?"

He drew back and scowled. "Don't ask silly questions."

Alice's shoulders drooped and she pouted at him.

He said, "Sorry about my temporary attack of madness. I'm much better now." He was looking at the ground. "Now where's my hat?"

Alice put one fist on her hip. "So what's so special about that hat?"

He was dusting it off and grinning. "This hat, my girl, is a very special, magical hat specifically designed for you!"

Alice squealed. "Ooh! Is it a gift for me?!"

"I made it just for you!" He held it out to her. "Put it on, why don't you!"

Alice slipped the hat on, but it was much too big for her 11-year-old noggin and slipped down to cover her eyes. Yet she didn't want to hurt the Hatter's feelings, so she made no mention of it, though she couldn't see a thing. "Thank you!" she exclaimed as chipperly as she could muster.

She felt the Hatter tapping the top of the hat, which only further pushed it down upon her face—why, the tip was resting on the end of her nose!

"Hey!" she exclaimed. *I shall soon have to mention the discrepancy of this hat's size!* she thought.

"There," said the Hatter, muttering more to himself than to anyone, it seemed. "The magic has been activated and focused on you. Your tears activated the magic."

"What do you mean?" said Alice. "I'm sorry, but I can't see a thing."

"Oh yes, I apologize. The hat is obviously much too big for you. I regret that you shall have to give it back. I shall wear it instead."

"Give it back?!" She lifted the hat so that she could see, and so that she could glare at him. "But you only just now gifted it to me!"

"Yes, my apologies, but what are you to do with an oversized hat? No, you must give it back. And as you do so, I would like you to recite something. A little poem."

"What poem?" she said suspiciously.

"Listen carefully so that you can recite it. It must be repeated exactly. I would like you to say these words:

"I give you this, my tuned in hat,
Encharmed with what my tears begat,
By carrying this gift, heartfelt and true,
You carry part of me with you."

Alice's jaws dropped slightly as she heard the words. "I daresay, those words are *quite* specific! Why, they almost sound like a spell!"

"A spell?" He laughed unconvincingly. "Ridiculous! I, um… Oh, don't make such trouble for me! Can't you just do this one thing for me, since I went to all the trouble to make this special hat for you?!"

"But you're taking it back!"

Suddenly Alice was regretting having been given the hat at all!

"Please?" said the Hatter, and Alice felt a surge of what? Power? Opportunity? For she rarely heard the Hatter say the P word, so he must *really* want her to say his little poem.

She thought for a way she could take advantage of the situation. "I want another hug," she said.

"Pardon?"

"If I say those words, I want you to give me another hug."

The Hatter raised his finger and opened his mouth to protest, then shut his mouth. "Is that all?"

"Quite."

"Very well," he said with a dismissive wave of his hand.

"Promise?"

"Yes."

"And not a short hug, but one of a reasonable length of time."

"Fine!"

"Very well then," said Alice. She took the hat off. "I'm afraid I didn't memorize the little speech. You'll have to lead me along."

So the Hatter fed the lines to her as she handed the hat to him. They were both holding onto it as they recited the lines.

The Hatter broke into a big grin. "Ah, there we are!" He set the hat atop his head. "It's all sorted then!"

"Yes," said Alice. "All except…" She tilted her head and fixed him with a leering grin. "You're too tall, so get on your knees, too."

He muttered, "Fine." He went down on his knees then he opened his arms and then they were embracing each other.

Alice held on tight. She smushed her cheek against his as he squirmed uncomfortably.

"This is nice," she said. "Isn't this nice? Mmmmm."

"It's better than being poked with a hot stick," he agreed.

Alice rocked him a little, reveling in the sensation of him in her arms. "Tell me…" she ventured, "Do you love me?"

"Why do you keep asking me that?"

"Because you never truly answer."

"Am I required to tell you so?"

Alice said, "I don't want you to say it if you don't mean it."

"Very well."

"Do you love me, Hatter?"

"I am…not repulsed by you."

Alice grinned big and kissed his cheek. He squirmed some more. She held him tight, hoping to hold on to this moment as long as she could.

ABOUT THE AUTHOR

Lotus, or Lotey, as he keeps trying to get people to call
him, lives in Austin, Texas, where he attended the
University of Texas at Austin. He invented the
corruptagram, a symbol he hopes will someday be
banned in public schools. He enjoys Newcastle Brown
Ale and gothic music.

His website is at~ loteyrose.com

Also by Lotus Rose, *Machoponi: A Prance with Death,* **the first book of The Poniworld Chronicles**

In this "children's book for adults," MachoPoni has no choice but to enter the Dark Kingdom, where the undead ponies roam. He must rescue Dust, the poni he loves from the dark princess's castle, using wit, creativity and his magic bouncy blue ball to survive.

A twisted parody of My Little Pony, The Care Bears, and other 80's staples. Warning: contains gore and mild sexual content.

Note: Other volumes in the Poniworld Chronicles are now available. They're called *Mein Poni-Kampf: A Biography of the Leader of the Nazi Ponies, My Brootal Poni: A Very Butch Poni Tale,* and *Dust in Your Eyes: An Erotic Poni Tale.*

Also by Lotus Rose, *SinEaster,* the book that started the Twisted Holiday Specials

Like a naughty Easter version of *The Nightmare Before Christmas* mixed with *Charlie and the Chocolate Factory*... On the day before her 18th birthday, Charlee wasn't expecting to be transported to Easter Land. A princess informs her she must compete to decide which of three creatures will be the future egg deliverer. But a man tied to a dark holiday known as SinEaster is also aware of her arrival.

For more info about all my books, visit http://loteyrose.com/bookinfo.html

Books by Lotus Rose

More info at <u>loteyrose.com</u>

The Corruption of Innocence, The Doll Queen, Poniworld Chronicles, Faerie Brace-Face Trilogy

Twisted Holiday Specials

SinEaster

Merry XXXmas, Charlee Frown

BlackHearts Day

Gothic Lolita Series

Gothic Lolita

Gothic Lolita 2: Heirloom

Gothic Lolita 3: Pageant

Malice in Wonderland Saga

Malice in Wonderland Prequel

Malice in Wonderland #1: Alice the Assassin

Malice in Wonderland #2: Alice the Angel of Death

Malice In Wonderland #3: Alice the Girl Who Will Tear Your Heart Out and Show It To You Before You Die

Malice Hates Fairy Tales Trilogy

Jabberwocky Trilogy

Dorothy vs. Alice Trilogy

www.ingramcontent.com/pod-product-compliance
Lightning Source LLC
Chambersburg PA
CBHW021059130626
46552CB00005B/2187